C
& NORTH-EAST SCOTLAND

The Dorothy Dunnett Guide

Jenny Myers

THE DOROTHY DUNNETT SOCIETY
Edinburgh
Dorothy Dunnett Society is a Scottish Charitable Incorporated Organisation No: SC030649
dorothydunnett.org

In memory of Dorothy Dunnett, who gave so much pleasure to so many.

There is no land uninhabitable or sea unnavigable.
(The Ringed Castle, *part 3, chapter 9)*

Contents

MAPS

Introduction

Of all her novels, Dorothy Dunnett considered *King Hereafter* to be her best work. Its historical and geographical compass is the nascent state of Scotland and the rôles Thorfinn II of Orkney and Macbeth of Moray played in its development. This guide covers all of eastern Scotland north of the River Dee and describes the places in the earldom of Orkney and Caithness and the mormaerdom of Moray which feature in this and her other books. The territories to the south (the kingdom of Alba, the principality of Cumbria and others) will be the subjects of future guides.

Most geographical names in Scotland are ancient, but over the centuries boundaries have changed, sometimes many times. In *King Hereafter*, Dorothy Dunnett's usage is appropriate to the 11th century and is matched in this guide.

The extensive area covered means this is a car-based guide, and whilst maps are provided to help readers visualise the geography, they are not detailed enough for navigation. Visitors will need good road maps and access to online or app mapping, as in-car navigation systems in this area are rarely helpful.

In Orkney, many place names are repeated and this can be confusing, as can the fact that the island where most of the action is set is called Mainland. In the guide it is capitalised with no definite article so, whilst the location of Kirkwall is Mainland, Thurso is found on the mainland of Scotland. 'Scotland' always refers to today's country.

Countryside or coastal walking is needed to reach a number of the locations and the same access law applies everywhere in Scotland. It allows responsible and thoughtful public access to land. Permission should be sought near farm buildings or homes. Readers should note that the many references to Rognvald that visitors see in Orkney cite, not the character in the book, but Earl Rognvald Kali Kolsson, great-grandson of Thorfinn II and founder of St Magnus Cathedral in Kirkwall in the 12th century.

There is much more to see in this part of Scotland, historical and otherwise, than is appropriate to include here and readers are encouraged to fully explore these beautiful areas.

History

Neolithic Orkney

Orkney's chief tourist attractions are its important prehistoric monuments, which new archaeological evidence shows are the UK's oldest. Several are referred to in the book and in Thorfinn's mind they were built by giants.

> *Not the family mound of one's ancestors ... but the mounds they said the first settlers from Norway had found, two hundred years since: the tombs of the giants who had built the great rings of Kjallar, of Odin, whose monoliths ... might walk ... down to the water to drink ... (*KH, *Pt 1, Ch 7)*

Bronze and Iron Ages Orkney

There are Bronze Age burial mounds at Brodgar and elsewhere, and Iron Age remains including brochs, the tall drywall towers mentioned several times in *King Hereafter*, are scattered around the islands.

Pictish Orkney

The Picts, immediate predecessors of the Norse in Orkney, inhabited the whole of east Scotland from Shetland to the Firth of Forth from approximately 300 BC to the 700s AD. The name Pict was used by the Romans for the Britons in areas that remained outside their empire and almost certainly is not what they called themselves. Rather than a single group, they were probably various groupings of native Iron Age Britons, but this is speculation. It is known that they spoke a Celtic language of the same type as Welsh and Breton and embraced the Christianity of St Columba between the 6th and 8th centuries. Indeed, the new churches built in Birsay by Thorfinn and Kirkwall by Rognvald both were on former Pictish sites.

What happened to these Britonnic people in Orkney is hotly contested in academia. There are two differing views – war or peaceful transition. Modern scholarship favours the former, with one theory proposing that, though the invasion of mainland Scotland was violent, the indigenous people there were ultimately absorbed into the new culture, but in Orkney they were exterminated and all trace lost.

Pictland, Alba and Moray

The sources indicate that 6th-century Orkney was subject to the Picts of mainland Scotland and it is assumed this continued into later times.

Roughly while the Picts were disappearing from Orkney under the pressure of the incoming Norse, the two loose agglomerations of kinship groups, sub-kings and high

7th/8th-century Pictish symbol stone

kings in Britonnic Pictland in the east and the Norse-Gael kingdom of Dál Riata in the west, were coming together as Gaelic-speaking Alba. The sources being scant and unreliable, there are differing views amongst historians as to how and when the merger occurred. Also matters of conjecture are the possibility that Pictland may have been two entities, north and south of the Mounth (see map p. 4), and the development of a semi-autonomous Gaelic-speaking Moray in the region that had been the domain of north Pictland. Genealogies suggest that Findlaéch mac Ruaidhí, father of Macbeth (or, as Dorothy Dunnett proposes in *King Hereafter*, stepfather of Thorfinn/Macbeth), was a member of the Cenél Loairn, a kinship group of Dál Riata which at times held the High Kingship of that kingdom. Their territory was at the south-western end of the Great Glen, and it is postulated that Findlaéch's ancestors invaded or migrated through the valley into the land of the Picts to form a power base which from time to time was a threat to an Alba that was ruled by a rival royal kinship group. Dorothy Dunnett's interpretation of the sources was that in Findlaéch's and his successors' time Moray was nominally subject to Alba but enjoyed a great deal of autonomy.

Norse Orkney and Northern Scotland

The complexities and gaps in the recorded history of medieval Scotland provide the very basis for Dorothy Dunnett's central premise in *King Hereafter* – that the historical Earl Thorfinn II of Orkney and Macbeth (Macbethad mac Findlaéch) King of Alba were one and the same person despite the discrepancy in their reported death dates of 1065 and 1057, respectively. By choosing this interpretation, the author is also choosing particular ways of knitting together various evaluations of conflicting and imprecise evidence. What follows, therefore, is a very brief summary of the extremely complex and scantily recorded historical background as interpreted by Dorothy Dunnett in her book.

> *King Olaf of Norway [was satisfied], he had laid the Orkneys under Norway again. The green, fertile islands with their mild climate and clever, boat-building peoples with the rich, bounding blood of the Picts and the Irish, the Norse and the Danes and Icelanders, to nourish their life-stream. Orkney, with its hundred small beaches and harbours: the crossroads where every merchant-ship rested, where every tax-boat and warship and supply vessel ran for shelter in the wild, open seaway between Norway and Viking cities of Ireland; between Norway and her colonies in the western isles, the ports of Wales and the markets of western England ...* (KH, *Pt 1, Ch 2)*

Here she has captured the complicated heritage and enviable qualities of the islands of Orkney. A major simplification is the minimal reference in the story to Shetland. Eighty miles to the north, Shetland was colonised at the same time as Orkney and was always part of the Norse earldom. When, as in *King Hereafter*, there were two or more incumbents at any given time, Shetland was part of the division of land between earls and in

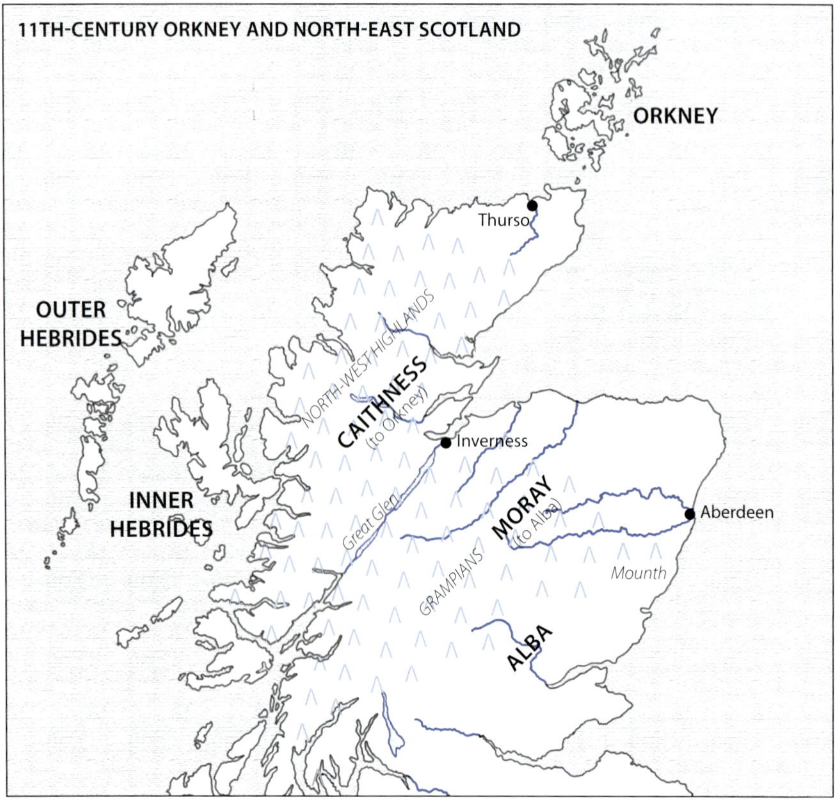

the story it was Rognvald's. This summary does not address its history.

When the first Norse arrived, probably in the 8th century, Orkney had been a fertile, cultivated land for 4,000 years or more. There is evidence that the island environment provided a wide range of food sources for a subsistence economy.

Before the end of the 9th century, and possibly earlier, the Norse in Orkney overran the north of Scotland, overturning the former relationship of subservience to the Picts there, and Caithness on the mainland became a client territory. At about the same time, the Norse were also establishing kingdoms in Dublin and north-east Ireland whilst pursuing their penetration and colonisation of the Sudreyar (Hebridean islands) and the mainland west coast and thus setting in motion the melding of Scandinavian and Celtic communities which created the Norse-Gael polities there, Dál Riata in particular.

The *Orkneyinga* saga describes the founding of an earldom subservient to his rule by Harald I (Fairhair) of Norway. For centuries afterward the earldom would either be independent or owe allegiance to the kings of Norway as circumstances dictated. Harald had sailed to Orkney and routed the pirates (*víkingar*) who were using Caithness and Orkney (the Nordreyar) as bases for raiding his country. However, the saga is a hagiography written several centuries later in Iceland and can be read as mythologising the origins of the earldom to provide it with a genealogy. The founding is on the edge of recorded history,

Stained glass images of Thorfinn and Thorkel, St Magnus Cathedral

and other source information, mainly Irish annals, is undated or subject to conflicting dates. The earliest reliable evidence is that Thorfinn II was the direct descendant of Einar Rognvaldsson (Turf-Einar), who was the first documented and, in legend, the fourth, earl. Earl Thorfinn's great grandfather, Thorfinn I (Skull-splitter), fathered four sons who all became earl in turn amidst familial internecine strife and the grandfather of Thorfinn, Hlodver, was the last of the brothers to become earl. Hlodver's son Sigurd was an extremely successful sea-warrior, who brought Caithness firmly under his control. His predation of the Hebrides (Sudreyar), south-western Scotland and Ireland hugely extended his domain and the *Orkneyinga* saga recounts Arnór's verse describing his son Thorfinn's prowess as a young man at sea maintaining Orcadian control in the west.

In the early years of the 11th century, the earldom of Orkney and Caithness and the kingdom of Alba, enemies or allies as the circumstances demanded, had both been in existence for some 150 to 200 years. Situated between them, the former territory of North Pictland had become the powerful mormaerdom of Moray.

Unsurprisingly, given their shared border, there are accounts of hostilities between Findlaéch, Mormaer of Moray, and Earl Sigurd of Orkney, and it was in the years immediately before Sigurd's death that the Orcadian Raven battle banner first appears in the sources. In Alba, Malcolm II had taken the throne in 1005 with total ruthlessness and for most of his reign was preoccupied with Cumbria and his southern neighbours, but he arranged marriages for his daughter(s) to the antagonists to his north. This, no doubt, provided a degree of security for Alba and possibly a lever to exploit the differences between his neighbours. Such marriages would offer similar advantages to Orkney and Moray. Sigurd already had three grown sons when Thorfinn was born of his Alban marriage to Bethoc. Most writers on the subject assume that Findlaéch of Moray's Alban royal wife was the mother of his attested son Macbethad and that she was a sister of Sigurd's wife. This interpretation makes cousins of the Orcadian and Moravian boys. Dorothy Dunnett, who did her own primary research, disagreed. She preferred not to assume the existence of an unattested sister and reached a different conclusion about the historical Thorfinn and Macbethad.

In 1014, leaving his older sons in charge of Orkney, Earl Sigurd went to fight in Ireland and died at the Battle of Clontarf. The three men now shared the earldom and Malcolm created an Alban earldom of Caithness and Sutherland for his five-year-old Alban/Orcadian grandson, even though the territory had already been annexed to the Orkney earldom. Some years after the eldest of the joint earls died, Thorkel Amundason, Thorfinn's foster-father, forced the remaining joint earls, Einar and Brusi, to accept his young charge's right of inheritance in Orkney. Thorkel's family home at Sandwick was in

Einar's territory and the animosity between them resulted in the earl's murder by Thorkel in 1020. Findlaéch of Moray was also murdered by a relative in about 1020, and it was these two acts that precipitated the visits of Thorkel Amundason, Earl Thorfinn and Earl Brusi to the king of Norway as described in the sources and used by Dorothy Dunnett in the opening chapter of *King Hereafter*.

More details of the history are given in 'Macbeth and his Origins' by Heike Meyer, published in 2012/3 across three issues (116–118) of *Whispering Gallery*, the magazine of the Dorothy Dunnett Society.

THE JOINT EARLDOM OF ORKNEY: SUMARLIDI, EINAR, BRUSI, THORFINN AND ROGNVALD

... because the pasture was rich enough ... the landed men ... of Orkney, were able to pay their Earl's winter tribute in food and malt from each ounceland which ... [kept] the Earl ... until the seas opened again in the spring-time. (KH, *Pt 1, Ch 16)*

The exact division of the territory of Orkney between the joint earls is not clearly defined in *King Hereafter* and indeed, Dorothy Dunnett gives at least two versions. It is known from the *Orkneyinga* saga that Einar's territory was eastern Mainland, which probably included the South Isles. Brusi's was the North Isles and Shetland, the inheritance of his son Rognvald. It is likely that Sumarlidi, the eldest, held western Mainland, which was subsequently won for Thorfinn by Thorkel. Thorfinn's portion contains the most fertile land and may have included the islands closest to Mainland off its north coast. It is not clear how this division was achieved or maintained but one theory is that it may have been based on the taxation system of pennylands and ouncelands, portions of land, steadings or settlements which raised a specific amount of income for the earl. Pennylands were the smaller units; 20 to an ounceland in Orkney. Using this system, it is the not the size of the territory that is of primary importance but the income it generates. Income which our author interprets as produce.

Brough of Deerness

Orkney

Mainland

Known in Viking times as Hrossey (Horse Island), Mainland is the largest island in the archipelago. Most of the locations in *King Hereafter* are here. In this guide it is divided into East and West, although Kirkwall is treated separately. Control of the two parts of the island changes hands several times during the course of the book, but boundaries are a matter for speculation. For example, Dorothy Dunnett puts Orphir in Rognvald's East Mainland territory, though it has not been possible to identify her source for so doing.

A Central Mainland

Kirkwall is an obvious place for a Norse settlement to develop. It is on the route from northern Scandinavia to Ireland and is situated where Mainland narrows, giving it easy access to south-facing beaches, such as at the head of Scapa bay.

> *... with Höfn fallen into disrepair and Orphir burned down, Earl Rognvald had moved his household to Kirkwall ... There was also a good enough harbour, except in north winds ... Best of all ... the new hall was Earl Rognvald's own idea, and had none of the pawmarks of the kindred on it. As the feeling of ownership grew on him, he had even begun to have a church built by the stream, and meant to dedicate it to St Olaf, which ought to please King Magnús and his uncle King Harald. (*KH, *Pt 2, Ch 11)*

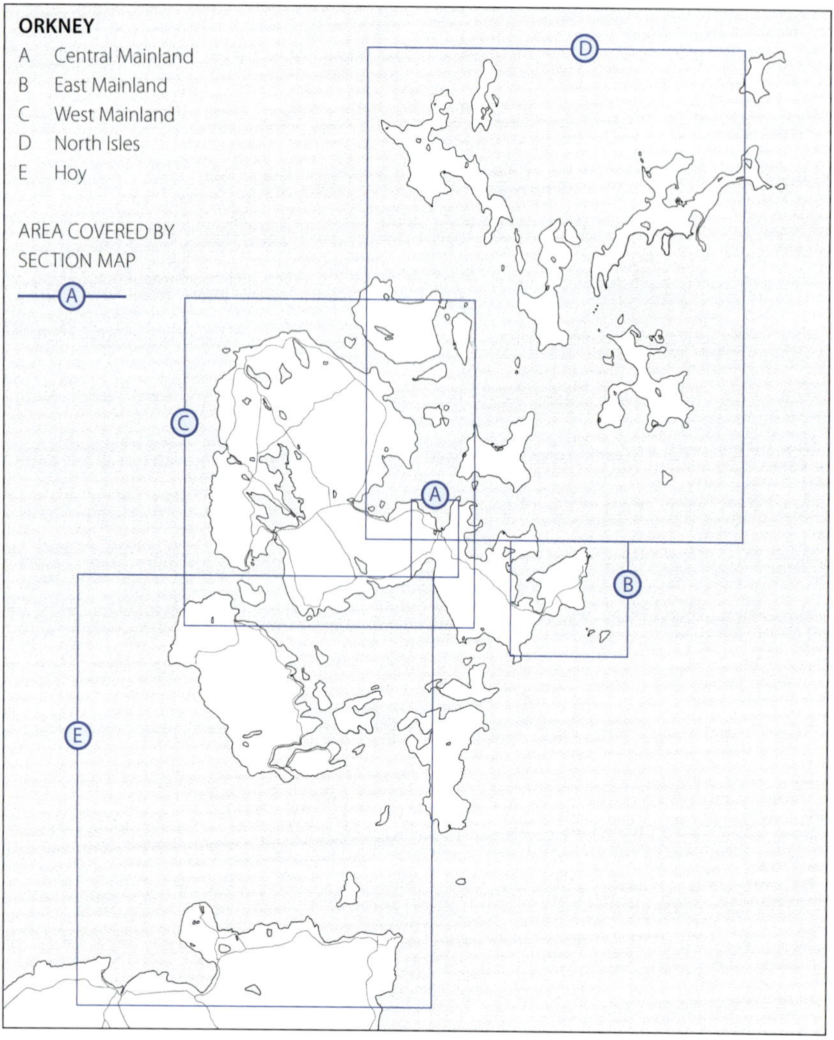

Orkney's capital is thought to date from the 11th century, when Rognvald's church was founded. The town's name ultimately derives from the Old Norse *Kirkjuvágr*, meaning church bay or inlet, and the church is the one referred to in the quote. Kirkwall grew in the area between the bay and the much larger body of water now known as Kirkwall Bay. Situated at the southern extremity of the larger bay, it was almost enclosed by an *ayre*, or shingle beach (Norse for 'rocky shore'), forming an *oyce*, or shallow body of water, that offered a safe harbour. Kirkwallians used these terms as proper nouns. The Ayre has been consolidated to now enclose the water, and it carries the Ayre Road out of town. The Oyce has become the Peerie or Peedie Sea and a model boat lake, but land reclamation has much reduced its size. The Viking harbour was both wider and longer.

A CENTRAL MAINLAND

1–8 Kirkwall, see p. 10
9 Lingro (Knarston)

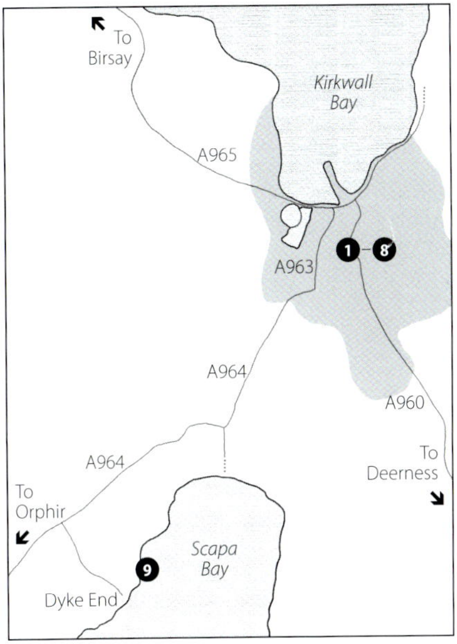

The earliest settlement consisted of traders' buildings in two rows, each approximately 90 m long. They made a corner with one row on the line of Bridge St facing the Oyce at the landward end of the shingle beach and the other facing the shore where today's Kirkwall Pier is situated. Rognvald's church (Loc 3) was built on the north bank of a stream which flowed east to west into the inlet, the Papdale Burn. 'Papdale' likely refers to a Pictish settlement of Papars, Celtic monks, that pre-dated the Norse in the valley.

Earlier in the book, Thorfinn returns to Orkney after his stay at Canute's court. He is now earl of two thirds of the territory and in possession of east Mainland. During his first winter, he is talking to Thorkel

> *... beside the new hall Thorfinn was building by the haven at Wall (*KH, *Pt 1, Ch 8)*

There is no settlement called Wall today. Dorothy Dunnett may be referring to North or South Walls (see map p. 35) or it may be fictional.

1 Bridge Street (possible site of Rognvald's hall)

> *... best of all ... the new hall was Rognvald's own idea, and had none of the pawmarks of the kindred on it (*KH, *Pt 2, Ch 11)*

Bridge St is the location of the Oyce-facing row of buildings in early Kirkwall. The eponymous bridge spanned the Papdale Burn at the junction with Albert St. The small river was mostly culverted years ago.

About halfway along Bridge St, a yard open to the street and now used as a car park was the site of a succession of prestigious homes. The last such house burned down in the 1930s. (The Groatie Hoose in the garden of the Orkney Museum (Loc 8) was originally here.) The first named owner dates to the 15th century. Given that rich men throughout the ages favoured high-status sites and that this one is near St Olaf's church (Loc 3), some sources speculate that both Rognvald's drinking hall (*skali*) and the much more elaborate home of his namesake Earl Rognvald Kali Kolsson were here.

Harbour St/Shore St (the general location of the north-facing early buildings) at the north end of the street is new, but Bridge St itself and its extension, Albert St, are the oldest surviving streets in the town.

KIRKWALL

1 Bridge Street (possible site of Rognvald's Hall)
2 Willow Burn (Papdale Burn)
3 St Olaf's Wynd (St Olaf's Kirk)
4 The Brig
5 St Magnus Cathedral
6 Bishop's Palace
7 Earl's Palace
8 Orkney Museum
--- 11th-century coastline

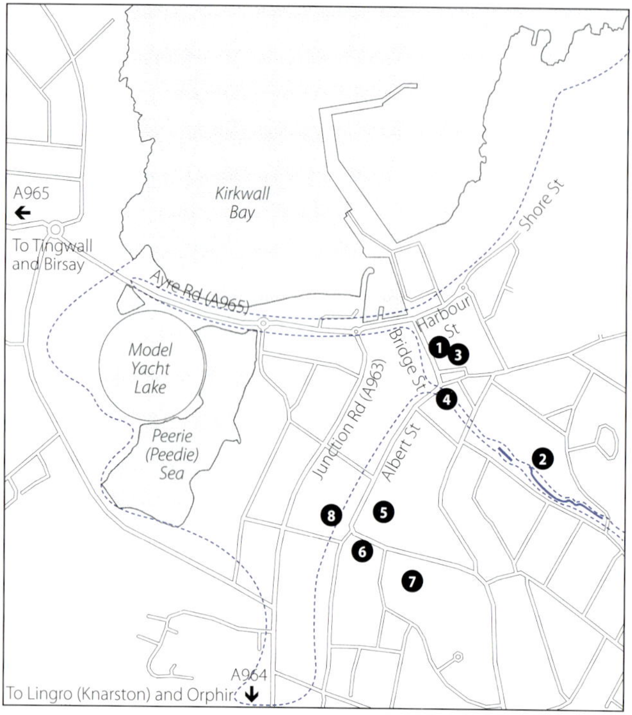

2 WILLOW BURN (PAPDALE BURN)

Papdale Burn still has short above-ground sections. One such, a few streets away to the south-east, is now named Willow Burn. Papdale House, the home of the Laing family, also stood in the area and is remembered in a group of 'Papdale' streets a little further east. The water continues to flow underground and it can be heard in Bridge St Wynd.

Burnmouth St, built on the reclaimed land to the west, commemorates the Papdale Burn meeting the Oyce.

3 St Olaf's Wynd (St Olaf's Kirk)

> *[Kirkwall] ... where there was a stream and the stumps and gravestones and midden of an old monastery.... he had ... begun to have a church built by the stream, and meant to dedicate it to St Olaf.* (KH, *Pt 2, Ch 11)*

The only indication of the approximate site of the church to which Kirkwall owes its name is the archway of cut stone that has been reconstructed and incorporated into a modern wall in St Olaf's Wynd. As in *King Hereafter*, the original church is thought to have been built by Rognvald Brusason. He dedicated it to his foster-father, King (Saint) Olaf. As intimated by Dorothy Dunnett, the church may not, in fact, have been a new building at all, but an earlier, possibly Pictish, religious building re-dedicated to St Olaf. Archaeology at the junction of St Olaf's Wynd with Bridge St has established that this is the site of the church's graveyard.

4 THE BRIG

The site of the eponymous bridge, the junction of Bridge St and Albert St, is known locally as the Brig, and on its south side is Parliament Close. A plaque on the wall of a building commemorates a Scottish parliament held there in 1540. It states that the site served the same purpose in Norse times, part of local folklore. By the 12th century, the power centre of Orkney had transferred here from Birsay and this site's proximity to St Olaf's church and the water of the Papdale Burn prompts scholars to agree this is a likely *thing* site. A *thing* in Norse societies was an outdoor parliament held at a dedicated site at which people could air grievances and earls would dispense justice.

St Magnus Cathedral

5 ST MAGNUS CATHEDRAL

The building of the cathedral, which stood on the firm ground nearest to the harbour inlet, began in 1137, a year after Rognvald Kali Kolsson claimed the earldom of Orkney, granted to him by the king of Norway. It is dedicated to his mother's brother Magnus Erlendsson, grandson of Thorfinn. Earl Thorfinn's sons Paul and Erlend had ruled jointly until their children's animosity caused the earldom to be, once again, divided into two territories. The animosity ended in the murder of Magnus in or around 1116 by his cousin Haakon Paulsson on Egilsay following a *thing* on Mainland.

6 BISHOP'S PALACE

This building's association with Bishop Robert Reid evokes a recollection of Lymond's trial at the end of *The Game of Kings*.

Inside the Tolbooth ... [the] Assize was preparing ... twelve assessors ... President of the Court of Session, Bishop Reid of Orkney with his deaf ear. (GoK, *Pt 4, Ch 4.2)*

It is likely that the original Bishop's Palace was built in the 12th century to house the first bishop of the new cathedral. In doing so, the Orcadians would be following the example of Trondheim in Norway, where a similar palace was erected when the cathedral there was rebuilt. By the 14th century, it was in ruins and possibly remained so until the 16th, when James V installed Robert Reid as Bishop of Orkney in 1541. Reid was subse-

Bishop's Palace, left, and Earl's Palace, right

quently appointed Lord President of the College of Justice, this time by Governor Arran. In this capacity, at the end of *The Game of Kings*, he passes judgement on Lymond. He reappears at the banquet given by the Comte de Sevigny at the Hôtel d'Hercule in *Checkmate* and is one of the members of the Scottish delegation to the wedding of Mary, Queen of Scots to the Dauphin who die from poisoning.

Reid was responsible for building the highly defensible round tower at the north-west corner, where he had his living quarters, and probably also the buttresses supporting the much older west wall of the palace. It is also thought that he had the basement of the hall vaulted.

7 EARL'S PALACE

This 17th-century palace, whose ruins represent one of the finest surviving examples of Scottish Renaissance architecture, was built by Patrick, son of the tyrannical Earl Robert Stewart, who built its counterpart at Birsay (Loc 27). It was intended to form a complex of buildings with the Bishop's Palace, but the plan was forestalled by Patrick's rebellion against King James VI. He was executed in 1615.

8 ORKNEY MUSEUM

Opposite the cathedral, the Orkney Museum's internationally important collection presents the history of Orkney from the Neolithic through the Pictish and Norse periods and up to the present day in a very accessible way. As a bonus there is a sheltered garden with seating. Also in the garden is the Groatie Hoose, a small 18th-century building thought to be have been built as a summer house. It was removed from the prestigious site in Bridge Street (Loc 1) and rebuilt in the museum garden stone by stone.

9 Lingro (Knarston)

Considering the benefits of Kirkwall as a base, Rognvald notes that, in addition to the north-facing harbour there, he has

> *... a back door to Knarston and the Flow that was not to be sniffed at ...* (KH, *Pt 2, Ch 11)*

The 'Flow' is Scapa Flow, the huge bay south of Kirkwall. It may be inferred that Knarston is a beaching site on the bay. To be of strategic value, it would need to be close to Kirkwall. There is no such settlement called Knarston here now, but it is mentioned in the *Orkneyinga* saga in an incident in which the protagonists were lying at Skálpeið, off Knarrarstaðir with thirteen ships. So where was it?

Scholars' best guess is Lingro, where there is a good bay for beaching boats by Mid Taing, south of the Scapa distillery. From the A964, take the road signposted the farmstead Dyke End, which is located by the sea. The bay is about 350 yards away to the left (north).

> 'Knarston' is derived from Old Norse for 'a mooring place for knarr cargoships', and yet Knarston near Dounby in West Mainland is one of several inland place names with seafaring etymological roots. New research evidence proposes the possible existence of a long-lost shallow Norse canal linking these places with Loch of Harray in the centre of the island and with Birsay to the west via intermediate lochs and a portage. It is believed that it may have been used to transport produce such as grain, collected as rents or taxes. If Dorothy Dunnett had known of this research, would she have had Thorfinn and Groa travel from Birsay to the farm at Brodgar (Locs 24/27 to 31) by boat?

B East Mainland

At its eastern end, Mainland narrows to an isthmus and beyond it is Thorkel's ancestral home of Deerness. It is where, returning from his years at the English court, Thorfinn tells his foster-father that Canute has successfully invaded Norway and he, Thorfinn, is now defender of all Orkney.

10 Skaill (Sandwick)

> *They were at Sandwick in Orkney ... preparing to hold Yule in the big hall that Thorkel Fóstri had inherited ...* (KH, *Pt 1, Ch 14)*

Thorkel's ancestral home of Sandwick is on the east coast of Deerness. The settlement there now is named Skaill, a name derived from the Norse *skali* (drinking hall). As with many Orkney sites, the names are repeated elsewhere on Mainland, but even if archaeological excavations here had not confirmed it as the Amundason family home, the many references in *King Hereafter* identify this as the site.

B EAST MAINLAND

10 Skaill (Sandwick)
11 Sandside Bay (Sandwick)
12 The Gloup
13 Brough of Deerness
14 Large Burra Geo (the bay next to Brough of Deerness)
15 Copinsay
16 Newark Bay
17 Dingieshowe Broch
- - - clifftop path
||||||| track

That winter, Thorkel visited his home at Sandwick, Orkney, for the first time since Earl Brusi held it. (KH, *Pt 1, Ch 7)*

At the beginning of *King Hereafter* King Olaf of Norway awards East Mainland to Earl Brusi. It had been the inheritance of his brother Einar, whom Thorkel had killed.

Thorkel's next move, everyone agreed, was a predictable one. He removed from life one of the joint Earls of Orkney. The chain of events which led up to the deed was quite complex, and the head of Earl Einar was cut off, in the event, by somebody else. (KH, *Pt 1, Ch 1)*

Excavation of Thorkel's hall: fireplace (left) and wall and bench

The Sea Battle against Carl Thorbrandsson off Deerness (*KH*, Pt 1, Chs 9 and 10)

At Brechin, Crinan suggests a plan to Gillacomghain to kill Thorfinn and install Gillagomghain's nephew Maddan as Earl of Caithness. It involves sending a fleet of eleven ships led by Carl Thorbrandsson of York to sail north from Buchan Ness, some of them out of sight of land, to surprise and engage Thorfinn's smaller fleet off Duncansby whilst Gillacomghain and Maddan march overland from Wick to engage his army.

Sulien overhears the plot and warns Thorfinn. After weeks of planning and informed by a signal, Thorfinn sails with his five ships east from Thurso in order to be seen by the ships from the south as they round Duncansby Head. Thorfinn turns and heads for Sandwick, drawing the larger fleet into Orkney waters. Arnór the skald is 'dumped' by skiff on the jetty at Sandwick, and the ships continue north, apparently intending to sail around the coast.

Instead, Thorfinn's ships sail straight out to sea for five minutes and then stop because they have dropped their sails. They use the oars to turn round to face the Northumbrian ships. Just then, as Thorfinn knows it will, the wind changes to his advantage. He also knows what effect the current will have.

The two fleets engage. Thorfinn wins the battle and claims Thorbrandsson's ship. Eight other Northumbrian ships sail back south and two are driven ashore to be redeemed later by 'David of Deerness and his family, who buried what they contained: the Northumbrian bodies in the turf and [jewellery] in the chapel ...'

The *Orkneyinga* saga describes this event as involving, not Carl Thorbrandsson, but the mysterious 'Kali Hundison, King of Scotland'. No one of that name is mentioned in any of the historical sources except the saga, but Dunnett finds a way to acknowledge the discrepancy. Sulien is with Lulach when he overhears the plotting of Crinan and Gillacomghain. As the men emerge from their meeting Sulien asks the child who they are. He dismisses Lulach's first answer of 'Macdowell' which he takes as applying to Crinan. He asks again, and again is given an unexpected answer: '"Kali Hundison"' '"No, it is your father. The nurse says it is your father,"' [says Sulien].

Gillaghomghain, Mormaer of Moray, is Lulach's father. So, while Dorothy Dunnett chooses Carl Thorbrandsson to fight the battle with Thorfinn she identifies Kali Hundison as one of the instigators of the attack.

Interpretations of Kali Hundison as 'King of Scotland' vary. One is that it refers to a 'high king', probably to a king of Alba and another that 'Mormaer' can be translated as 'king' of his territory. In this conversation Dorothy Dunnett chooses the latter.

It has not been possible to uncover Dorothy Dunnett's reason for having Lulach give the name Macdowell to Crinan. One possibility is that she had evidence that he was from a Norse-Gael family in Galloway where the name may have originated.

The *Orkneyinga* saga tells us that the murder took place at Sandwick and Thorkel was obliged to travel to Norway to receive exculpation from King Olaf.

11 Sandside Bay (Sandwick)

On the evening of Thorfinn's return from Canute's court with news of the death of King Olaf, Thorkel seeks some respite from the homecoming festivities.

> *... the great hall at Sandwick ... during the feasting ... he had to leave [and stand] under the moon ... where ... the salt tang and hush of the sea drew him away from the heat and the noise above the beach and along the high ground from where, looking over the ocean, he could discern ... ahead, the glimmering fire on Deerness, joy-beacon, dying now on the wind, to celebrate the death and defeat of a king.* (KH, *Pt 1, Ch 8)*

Thorkel has walked a little way north along the bayside and is looking toward the Gloup (Loc 12) and the Brough of Deerness (Loc 13). Among the features found when the Amundason longhouse was excavated and reburied in the 1960s were the walls, stone benches and fireplace (where Einar was killed). The hall stood in the area between the road and sea which can be seen from the gate at the north end of the barn. About 500 yards further along the road is a sharp bend in the road and a track leading to the beach. Depending on the tide, you may see the Skerries of Skaill which Carl Thorbrandsson knows to avoid when preparing to fight Thorfinn.

> *... a strange fleet sailing north in such numbers was not likely to be a friendly one ... Thorfinn could choose to run for the shore and risk being overwhelmed and his five ships burned where they lay ... Or he could fight at sea ... Carl Thorbrandsson knew better ... than to cut straight across Sandwick and intercept the Caithness men there. There were skerries opposite Sandwick, and more you couldn't see, under the water ...* (KH, *Pt 1, Ch 10)*

It is thought likely that there was a Christian chapel associated with the hall here. St Ninian's Kirk, near the domestic buildings, possibly stands on the same general site. A hogback tombstone dated to the late 11th or 12th century was found in the graveyard in the 1700s and is now kept in the Session House attached to the church.

12 The Gloup

Precipitating the events that end the book, Thorkel persuades his foster-son to go for

The Gloup and, below, inside the Gloup

a sail and, unaware of Thorfinn's battle injuries and wanting to go fowling, takes the boat into the Gloup.

> *... the Gloup, a sea-tunnel half exposed to the sky ... [Thorfinn] did take both oars and three or four strokes were enough. Then they were ... under the arch of the sea-cave ... Beyond, the sunlight from a long-fallen roof showed how the river of sea flowed surging and slapping between the continuing walls of the chasm: on the left, sheer, towering rock, and on the right, a broken wall nearly as steep, but bearing rock-plants and lichen spilling down to its ledges from the sandy pastures over its rim ... the water slapped the walls and fell back with an echoing gurgle that had earned the place its name ...* (KH, *Pt 4, Ch 15)*

This collapsed sea-cave is approximately 36 m long and 24 m deep. There are two open portions divided by a wide land bridge. The rock formations and vegetation described in the quote can still be seen on the landward portion, though it is even better if you can find someone to take you in by boat. The seaward portion can be seen from the path which takes you to the sea, if you care to go that close to the edge.

If you are lucky enough to get in by boat, you will also be able to confirm that:

> *... the sea-inlet ran on into darkness ... until ... a shelf of pebbles showed you ... where the way was finally blocked.* (KH, *Pt 4, Ch 15)*

The Gloup is a short walk from the Mull Head Nature Reserve car park. Its name comes from Old Norse for chasm – *gluppa*.

13 Brough of Deerness

The brough is a thirty-metre-high rocky outcrop where Thorkel waits to hear whether Canute of England has successfully annexed Norway.

> *... [He] chose to await his fate on the sacred green prow of Orkney, the monks' cliff of Deerness ... the monks ... had built their huts in the sun, above the terns and the seals, on this God-made tower of layered pink rock, chained to the gulleys and pools of the mainland by rotting spines of pebble and stones. [...]*
>
> *[He] looked up and saw ... a single square sail, low on the horizon to the east ... a longship ... [with] the banner that beat like a black bird of prey ... In all the*

world there were only two living men entitled to fly the black raven of Sigurd of Orkney ... 'It is the Earl Thorfinn' ... (KH, *Pt 1, Ch 8)*

Chapel, Brough of Deerness

Access to the brough is via a steep and narrow path, much as it must have been in the 11th century. Now there is a chain railing in places, but you need to descend from the cliff top to sea level via wooden steps to reach the beginning of the path. Set amongst the grass, the remaining walls of the 10th–12th century Norse chapel are tall enough to give a good idea of the structure, and there are traces of thirty or so other buildings. It is now thought that in later phases of Viking settlement it was a defensive structure and that its history may prove more complex. Further archaeological investigation may lead to more insights. However, the chapel is one of the earliest examples of Viking Christian sites, and the Norse buildings seem to have been built over earlier Pictish structures.

14 Large Burra Geo (the bay next to Brough of Deerness)

In *King Hereafter* there is a small religious community on the brough and only a single monk, David Hvita, who lives here with his family and who acts as scribe for the illiterate Thorkel Fóstri. They stand together, watching as Thorfinn's longship approaches. Thorkel moves to return to his father's home and the monk tells him

'... I think the longship has turned for this bay'.

Leaping down to the beach, with the little settlement emptying behind him ... Instead of a clean half-moon of blue pebbles, the beach was thick as a bere-field with heads ... of married women ... young girls ... farmers ... (KH, *Pt 1, Ch 8)*

Large Burra Geo

Here in this small bay with grey-blue pebbles, Thorfinn addresses the crowd.

His voice rolled and boomed, even in that

Bird cliffs, Copinsay

open space, as if it came from the cauldrons of the underworld, and along the beach, men replied with the voices of gulls. (KH, *Pt 1, Ch 8)*

He announces that King Olaf is dead, that Canute is King of Norway and that Rognvald has gone back to Novgorod.

15 Copinsay

Thorfinn and Thorkel launch a boat from the beach at Sandwick to go fowling on the cliffs on the island of Copinsay to the south-east, crossing 'the channel of smooth, swelling sea.'

... Copinsay was a steep, turfy island girded with bird-ledges. They ran the boat up the shore, but avoided the farm ... instead they climbed up past the barns and out to the right, to the south-eastern rim of the island, where the cliffs were ... Round the rock-foot, the sea creamed ... They emptied the flask, and then went climbing.

The fowling cliffs ran for a mile and were made of red flagstones, split vertically into geo and notches and chimneys, and layered across like a shield-maker's stack-yard, From their green tops to the sea-shattered rocks at their base was a fall of two hundred feet. (KH, *Pt 1, Ch 8)*

Now uninhabited, the island is owned by the Royal Society for the Protection of Birds and is a Special Protection Area. Visiting in nesting season may result in being dive-bombed by Arctic terns! The island is wedge-shaped, sloping from the cliffs on the seaward side down to Thorfinn's and Thorkel's landing place near the now-abandoned farm steading that stands on a mound which archaeologists believe may be a Norse site. The nesting ledges on the cliffs can only be seen from a boat.

16 NEWARK BAY

One of the largest Pictish/Norse cemeteries in Scotland is part of ongoing archaeological study at the east end of the bay. There is evidence of a 10th-century chapel and of pre-Christian burials which may have been associated with the housestead at Sandwick. The analysis of one skeleton has indicated that it is of a seaman who rowed with his back to the direction of travel and often dragged his vessel overland!

17 DINGIESHOWE BROCH

Next to the beach on the small shallow Dingieshowe Bay on the south coast of Deerness is an Iron Age broch that dates from about 300 BC and sits on top of a Neolithic structure 700 years older than that. Its name, though, is Old Norse – *þingeiðshaug* (assembly-isthmus-mound) – and it is thought to be the *thing* site in East Mainland that was used by Earl Einar and therefore was where Thorkel spoke out against the earl's excessive taxes in the dispute which ended in murder in his family's hall.

C West Mainland

West Mainland is the third of Orkney which, throughout the book and without question, belongs to Thorfinn.

18 TINGWALL BROCH

This was the *thing* site for west Mainland and, though not mentioned in *King Hereafter*, it was almost certainly used by the historical Thorfinn the Mighty.

The meetings were probably held on this large ancient stepped mound next to the road to the Tingwall ferry terminal. Those meeting here would be able to see and be seen from Rousay, Egilsay and Wyre, the islands just to the north, which seem to have been part of same domain.

Birsay

For many centuries and for different cultures, the north-west parishes of Birsay and Harray had a special status. Their names derive from the first and second parts of the Old Norse name of Thorfinn's place of residence – *Birgisherað*. The second element of this terminology imputes a district associated with an important earldom centre. Archaeology shows that the area, in common with the rest of the archipelago, has been in continuous occupation for some 5,000 years. A high proportion of Orcadians are direct descendants of the Norse settlers. In Birsay, it is even higher.

Thorfinn chooses Birsay as his main residence. He has two halls here; he builds a church and fortifications. He keeps longships in the bay. The uncertainties of the archaeology make it difficult to identify specific sites, but Dorothy Dunnett embraces those uncertainties in her use of the Birsay sites. She locates what she wants where she wants them: some on Mainland and some on the brough, a tidal island accessible on foot across a causeway. The journey to Orphir, which is interrupted by Rognvald's kidnap of Groa (see panel p. 27), begins at Birsay but our author does not specify exactly where.

19 Bay of Birsay

> *Once, before the ocean broke through the neck of it, the island of Birsay had been the north horn of a wide bay where the new boats lay trim in their nousts.* (KH, *Pt 4, Ch 14)*

Nousts were trenches scraped out of the sand and surrounded by low walls of peb-

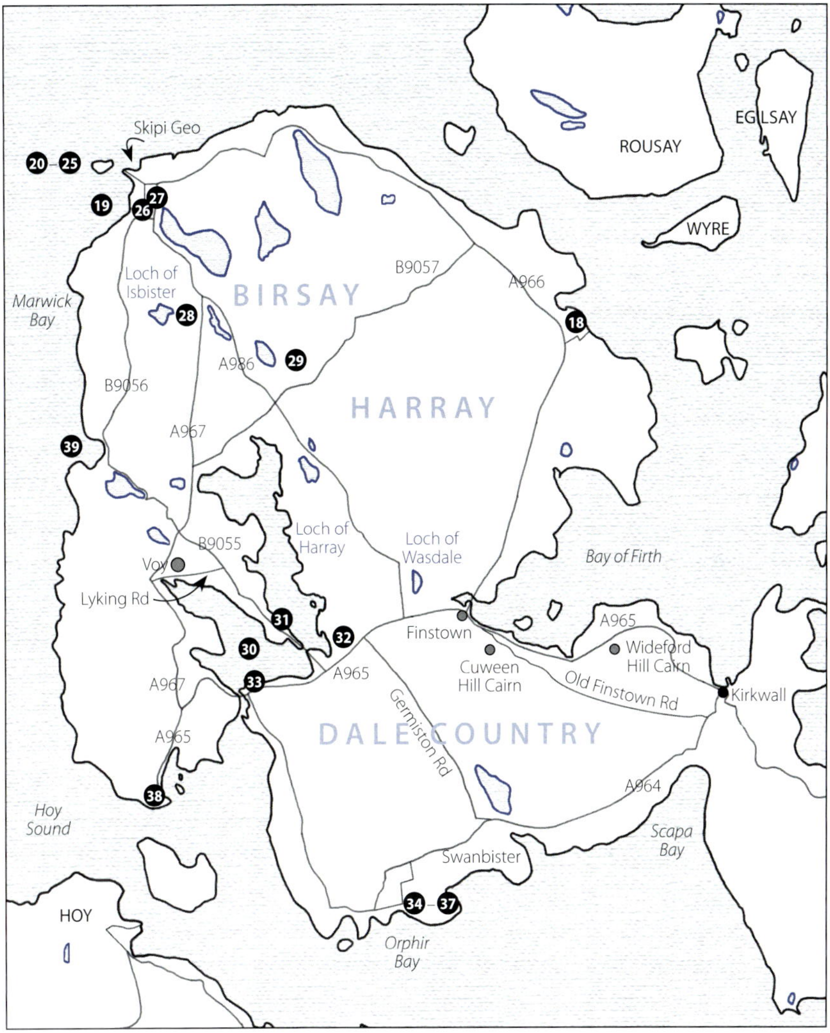

C WEST MAINLAND

18 Tingwall Broch

Birsay:

19 Bay of Birsay

20–25 Brough of Birsay, see p. 23

Birsay Village:

26 St Magnus Church

27 Earl's Palace (Thorfinn's Mainland hall)

28 Isbister

29 Beaquoy

30 Loch of Stenness

31 Ness of Brodgar

32 Maeshowe

33 Unstan Cairn

Orphir:

34 Orkneyinga Saga Centre

35 Earl's Church

36 Bu' (the drinking hall)

37 The stream and beach

38 Stromness

39 Bay of Skaill

bles and stones. They were made on the edge of the beach where boats could be easily hauled into them. Their obvious usefulness for launching quickly was counterbalanced by their vulnerability to Orkney's notorious weather, as demonstrated by Dorothy Dunnett's description of the storm in which

Nousts at Skipi Geo

> *At Birsay, no boat left in the nousts had survived.* (KH, *Pt 4, Ch 2)*

Although there are no longer any nousts at Birsay Bay, there are still some at several sites above the beaches of Mainland. These include Marwick Bay and Skipi (or Skiba) Geo. The latter is signposted from the car park for the Brough of Birsay (Locs 20–25) at Buckquoy Point and is a pleasant short walk along a cliff-top path.

Brough of Birsay

> *Like Deerness, it had been a place of safety sought by many peoples. There was a broch still on its far tip and there had been a Christian church and a Christian cemetery where now stood his new church ...* (KH, *Pt 4, Ch 14)*

The Pictish and Norse archaeological remains are situated in the north-east corner, nearest the Mainland. The ground slopes up to forty-metre cliffs in the west where there is a solar-powered lighthouse, but no Iron Age broch.

> *They spent Yule in Orkney, where Thorfinn was fortifying the near-island at Birsay* (KH, *Pt 1, Ch 13)*

Causeway to the Brough of Birsay

According to the *Orkneyinga* saga, Earl Thorfinn made the brough virtually his permanent home. This was unusual in medieval times when earls were generally peripatetic. It is a highly defensible site and

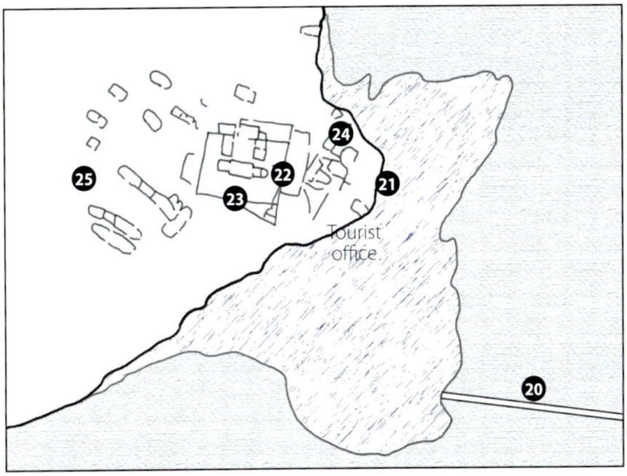

BROUGH OF BIRSAY

20 The causeway
21 The slipway
22 The church
23 The cemetery
24 Later Norse buildings
25 Early Norse buildings
Rocks

it is now thought that this was its chief use by Earl Thorfinn, although there are no remnants of defences evident.

20 The causeway

> *... from their old hall on the shore opposite Birsay [Thorfinn and Groa] walked across the causeway to the island with Bishop Jon ...* (KH, *Pt 3, Ch 12)*

Today the 250-metre causeway is part concrete path and part flattish rocks and shingle. It is only usable for two hours either side of low tide. Tide tables are available online.

21 The slipway

Visitors still arrive on the island at the slipway, which used to be much wider than it is now. In the book, though just renewed, it was 'broken with rocks' (*KH*, Pt 4, Ch 2) in the same storm that destroyed all the boats. Later, Thorfinn and Sulien arrive by boat at the

> *... long slipway that led up through the cliff-rocks to the settlement and his new hall and church.* (KH, *Pt 4, Ch 14)*

22 The church

> *... [Thorfinn, Groa, their sons and Bishop Jon] inspected the low walls that were all that could be seen of the old Pictish chapel and its boundary-stones ...*
>
> *In the event, the church which was to be ... [the] bishop's seat of Christ Church in Birsay occupied a good deal of the King's time that winter ... Groa explained 'They're rebuilding the church of the old Pictish monastery'.* (KH, *Pt 3, Ch 12)*

Its size and shape are still easily discerned with its circular apse at the eastern end. As the new building is shown to Sulien, we are given dimensions:

*Thorfinn said, 'We built in the same place, since it was holy. As you see, the church is small'. There were only fifty-five feet of it, in squared stones, carefully mortared. A rectangular nave, and a narrow choir, with an apse on the east side. Since the gale, the tower had never been rebuilt. Inside, it was sweet and clean, with fresh rushes in the nave and the smell of new carpentering. A plain cloth lay on the stone altar ... those [objects] necessary for the Mass were in their places, and within the altar, in the box made to fit it, the first banner Thorfinn had brought back ... blessed by the Pope and sanctified at the tomb of St Peter ... There was a bench along one wall ... (*KH, *Pt 4, Ch 14)*

There is debate amongst the experts as to whether the church had a tower. In *King Hereafter* it did, but in the same storm that damaged the slipway and in which Thorfinn's fleet was smashed,

*... the tower of his new church, its mortar still wet, had staggered and fallen. (*KH, *Pt 4, Ch 14)*

The dating of the Norse remains on the brough has been revised in recent years so that the current prevailing view amongst archaeologists agrees with Dorothy Dunnett's that the church was built on an earlier Pictish site, but in the early 12th century, after Thorfinn's time. Historians have hypothesised that Thorfinn's church may have been an interim building. When *King Hereafter* was written, the commonly held view was that the church had a double dedication, and Thorfinn tells Sulien:

*'Bishop Jon dedicated the church for us,' he said. 'To Christ and St Peter'. (*KH, *Pt 4, Ch 14)*

Some experts now believe that this church was dedicated to St Peter, whilst Thorfinn the Mighty's Christchurch, the seat of the Bishop, was in what is today's Birsay village (Loc 26).

23 The cemetery

*Outside the church was a grave-marker from the old cemetery, with the spider-drawings you saw by Forres and Glamis, and the disdainful eagle, and three stalking figures in Assyrian robes with their square shields and their spears. (*KH, *Pt 4, Ch 14)*

The original grave-marker stone is fragile and now in the National Museum of Scotland in Edinburgh (right). A replica, itself heavily eroded and difficult to make out, has been placed just inside the cemetery wall. The carved symbols identify it as Pictish, as does Dunnett in her reference to settlements in Moray where there are many more Pictish symbol stones, but the significance of the figures is uncertain.

24 Later Norse buildings

Thorfinn has recently returned from Rome and he and Groa have escorted the new Bishop through Scotia to Orkney for the winter. They arrive at the brough, and Groa tells Arnór,

Sauna, Brough of Birsay

'And now ... they've decided to knock down part of Earl Sigurd's hall and build a better one. With heating-flues, and a water-channel, and a bath-house outside. They are to rebuild the slipway ...' (KH, *Pt 3, Ch 12)*

The remains of 10th- and 11th-century Norse houses, some layered over one another, include a possible 'sauna' and a house with ducts for underfloor heating. These are now on the cliff edge as land erosion has claimed parts of the settlement. The site is, nevertheless, one of the best and most extensive Norse sites in Orkney. Even though current archaeological opinion does not exactly match the remains to Thorfinn's dates in *King Hereafter*, he is mentioned on some of the information boards.

Somewhat separated from the rest of the remains is what is thought to be a smithy. Smiths were responsible for creating weapons and decorative and ritual/religious objects in medieval society. Their skills were highly valued and often regarded as magical. The presence of a smithy here indicates a settled and high-status population. Dorothy Dunnett does not mention a smithy at Birsay, but at Inverness just after Thorfinn has bedded Groa he finds Sulien:

> *... in the smithy, deep in talk with two other churchmen while the smith patched an abbot's sword and put an edge back on their knives.* (KH, *Pt 1, Ch 11)*

25 Early Norse Buildings

A short distance up the slope are the remains of 9th- and 10th-century buildings which demonstrate a simpler form of Viking longhouses. They have low benches on either side of the fireplace and are of the same type as the hall at Sandwick (Loc 10), as described in the *Orkneyinga* saga, in which Earl Einar was murdered by Thorkel.

26 Birsay Village – St Magnus Church

Archaeological evidence may point to the site of this small church, rather than the brough, as the location of Thorfinn's cathedral called Christchurch, built circa 1064. Now dedicated to St Magnus, the medieval church dedicated to Christ was the first repository of the body of Earl (Saint) Magnus, who was a grandson of Thorfinn. The miracles which led to his canonisation began here, and this area became a place of pilgrimage and remained so after the Reformation. In the late 12th century, the saint's remains were removed and re-interred, at first in St Olaf's church in Kirkwall (Loc 3) and then in the newly built cathedral there (Loc 5). The church was closed in 1996 and is now run by the St Magnus Church Birsay Trust who make it available for viewing every day.

27 Birsay Village – Earl's Palace (Thorfinn's Mainland hall)

The palace, now a ruin, was built by Earl Robert Stewart, an illegitimate half-sibling of Mary, Queen of Scots. Archaeology suggests that this was also the site of Thorfinn's Mainland hall.

28 Isbister

At the start of the kidnap journey (see panel p. 27)

> *They had passed Isbister ...* (KH, *Pt 2, Ch 6)*

The loch of that name cannot be seen from the road. A track and bungalow on the A967 about half a mile from the junction with the A986 provide a marker.

29 Beaquoy

On that same journey, the travellers' first intimation that Rognvald is approaching is

> *... when they saw the dancing flares to the east, beyond Beaquoy ...* (KH, *Pt 2, Ch 6)*

This is a settlement on an access-only road.

30 Loch of Stenness

After joining their party on the way to Orphir, Rognvald is riding in Groa's sledge, and she tells him

> *'The Loch of Stenness has frozen, and the family at Brodgar have invited us to an ice-feast'.* (KH, *Pt 2, Ch 6)*

A sea loch, this body of brackish water is connected to the freshwater Loch of Harray to its north at the Bridge of Brodgar. It is not possible to reach the Stenness lochside at Brodgar, but the extent of the loch can be seen from the Lyking Road at Voy. Beyond the loch, the rising ground that is dale country can be clearly seen. There is another view of the loch from the Unstan Cairn (Loc 33).

31 Ness of Brodgar

The Ness is the tongue of land between the Lochs of Stenness and Harray. Some of the major tourist sites in Orkney are here: the Neolithic Standing Stones of Stenness and Ring of Brodgar and the ongoing archaeological dig, where finds are overturning previous theories of Neolithic Britain.

Rognvald's kidnapping of Groa begins at Brodgar. As the cavalcade approaches from

The Kidnap (*KH*, Pt 2, Chs 6 and 7)

... after sundown one afternoon ... they were travelling in torch-lit cavalcade from Birsay to Orphir.

Late on a snowy winter's day Thorfinn and Groa leave Birsay with their household to celebrate Yule at Orphir. They notice Rognvald's approach when his flares are seen as he rides from the east. He intercepts them and shares Groa's sledge until they reach the frozen loch and farmstead with its welcoming bonfire. After the feast Groa sits on the lochside while Thorfinn races on the ice with his men. She is waiting for them to reappear from the dark when she is forcibly removed and put into a sledge harnessed to a horse that Rognvald rides away from the farm towards the east. Approaching a stream that will overturn the sledge, Groa severs the harness and, as the sledge slows and stops, Rognvald leaves it and continues to ride eastwards. Thorfinn and Thorkel, chasing after, reach Groa who returns to the farm with Thorkel. Her husband, following Rognvald, is led across country on an eccentric route. He crosses a stream (the same stream?), rides over a rise and wheels down

to the flat, frozen face of another loch ... loop[s] round again, and for a moment [sees] far away and a little below him a circle of flares in the darkness ... and a single light, travelling swiftly, making towards it.

It is unlikely that Dorothy Dunnett has a specific route in mind here but, rather, evokes the Orcadian countryside by mentioning general and distinct geographical features. The 'flat, frozen loch' might be Loch of Harray or the small Loch of Wasdale. Thorfinn is looking down and back towards Brodgar and sees Thorkel and Groa returning to the farm. He passes two farmsteads and the

... trail swung wide, and he went on ... to the east ... [on] into the dale country of ... low hills ... [where] only the mounds of the dead where the haug-búi *watched.*

The narrative of the pursuit is interrupted here by Thorfinn's thoughts, which are themselves brought to an abrupt end by Rognvald's spear, thrown at his horse.

... [A] casting-spear flashed, once, in the light of his torch ... [Thorfinn's] horse fell ...across him ... [and] the bone snap[ped].

Lying on the ground, his leg broken by the horse's body, Thorfinn realises that his nephew is looking down on him from the top of a grave-mound.

... Rognvald, still mounted, picking his way delicately from the further side of a grave-mound to its top ... [Two more spears arrived and Thorfinn] screamed again

with the full power of his great voice, and on top of the mound Rognvald's horse, alarmed, trampled ... he saw Rogvnald drop from the saddle with a cry that became suddenly hollow, then stopped ... he could not see Rognvald ... only the unbroken white globe of the mound, and the threshing black bulk of the horse at its foot.

Thorfinn drags himself up to the edge of the hole into which the other man has fallen and, seeing Rognvald lying unmoving on the floor below, lets himself down to join him.

When Thorkel arrives the following morning, both men are taken on horseback back to Brodgar. From there Rognvald returns to his territory in the east and Thorfinn and Groa continue their journey to Orphir, approaching the hall from the west.

Given the break in the narrative which complicates any sense of distance the reader may have, and despite the fact that the direction of travel seems to remain broadly east, it is not possible to be definitive about where the cairn may be. The grave-mound the author describes is a chambered cairn and Cuween Hill Cairn and Wideford Hill Cairn both, broadly, fit the bill, though both are on hills which do not feature in the narrative. They are free to visit and open every day. Access to the former is an often muddy three-metre crawl and to the latter is via a ladder from a hatch in the roof. A torch is needed at both.

the north-west, the housestead is beyond the lights of flares and fire.

*Ahead, the night had become brilliant with fire: a ring of flares ended beside a vast bonfire that lit the low walls and the barns and sleeping-quarters and drink-hall of a big steading ... (*KH, *Pt 2, Ch 6)*

After the feast, Groa sits on the lochside whilst the men make sport on Loch of Stenness.

[The men] bound the polished bones on to their boots and pushed off on to the loch with their double sticks.

*... weaving and inter-weaving across the white field of the lake that vanished west into darkness while, to the north, high on the ridge between lakes, the great ring of monoliths [which] lent its nearer stones now and then to familiar fires. (*KH, *Pt 2, Ch 6)*

Ring of Brodgar

Dorothy Dunnett does not definitively locate the farm of the family at Brodgar, but this description places the gathering in the vicinity of the stone circle, with the bonfire between the steading and the Ring. 'Brodgar' means 'farm at the bridge/crossing' and the present farmhouse there (it has two standing stones outside it) is an unexcavated archaeological site. It is reasonable to assume that our author has used it. In that case, the bonfire might have been on the site of the archaeological dig!

32 Maeshowe

This large Neolithic cairn is almost certainly Dorothy Dunnett's model for the place in which the injured Rognvald and Thorfinn end up at the end Groa's kidnapping, as it contains the features she describes.

> *Fifteen feet below him, [Rognvald] was lying, and the glitter of blood from the great wedge-shaped rock slab beside him ... the disposition of the stones which provided the stepped roof of the beehive ... If he could cling to one of these and it did not give way, he might manage to had himself down, partly at least ... In the event he did not have to drop the whole fifteen feet ... [it was] a burial chamber built of mighty squared blocks, with high wall recesses leading to side chambers. The block of stone that had caused Rognvald's injury had been the block-door to one of these chambers, tumbled aside centuries ago by the first robbers ... [There was] a passage that he saw ran out, low and narrow, under the hill to one side.* (KH, *Pt 2, Ch 7)*

Though its geographical position does not fit the narrative of the kidnap, runic graffiti inside the chamber, which are also mentioned in the *Orkneyinga* saga, are evidence that it was, indeed, visited by Norsemen. Maeshowe can only visited in small groups. Advanced booking is required.

33 UNSTAN CAIRN

This cairn, situated at the south end of the Loch of Stenness, is also not a candidate for the one in the narrative, but it still may be of interest because the cement replacement roof includes glazing so that a torch is not needed. Though not as low as some, the entrance is nearly 8 m long. It includes features of both a chambered cairn, as in *King Hereafter*, and a stalled cairn, which are usually two distinct types. It is free and open all year.

Orphir

34 ORKNEYINGA SAGA CENTRE

The entrance to the extensive site is marked by a sculpture of a Viking longship outside an unprepossessing building which houses a very interesting exhibition and information centre based around the *Orkneyinga* saga.

35 EARL'S CHURCH

The remains are of the only Round Kirk in Scotland. It stands in a cemetery (kirkyard) that belonged to the (now vanished) 18th-century parish church, which was built using stones from the Norse building which had survived almost intact until then. Still standing is the round apse and a small portion of the circular nave, which was about 6 metres in diameter. Its floor, some steps and a stone altar are hidden about a metre below today's ground level.

Earl's Church

The church dates to the time of Earls Haakon and Magnus at the turn of the 11th and 12th centuries. It was dedicated to St Nicholas and is said to have been built by Earl Haakon Paulsson on his return from the pilgrimage to Rome that he undertook after his murder of his cousin Earl (St) Magnus Erlendsson.

36 Bu' (the drinking hall)

Bu' is a placename that indicates a large estate and it is known that this one belonged to the earldom. The hall is described in *King Hereafter* as standing among other buildings, and there are indications of a smithy on sloping ground next to the sea where a stream flows into Orphir Bay. Today there are many features in addition to a hall, but only foundations remain.

Just before she notices Rognvald's arrival on the night he has come to kill, Groa's slave

Remains of Bu'

Sinna looks out over the complex:

Orphir lay still on the slopes of its hill, but after hut black on the grey, save only the long shape of the drinking-hall with its amber rectangles of flickering membrane. (KH, *Pt 2, Ch 11)*

The site is extensive, but there are no detailed descriptions so it is not easy to work out what you are seeing. There were probably several iterations of the hall and this one must post-date the events in the book. Dorothy Dunnett's description of Rognvald's firing of the hall is derived from that of her source material – the *Orkneyinga* saga – which refers to the proximity of the later church.

37 The stream and the beach

After noting the glimmering windows of the hall amid the other dark buildings

> *[Sinna] could hear the stream that ran down to the shore, and the breath of the sea washing the shores of the Flow, and sense rather than see the low black islands that lay out there over the water ...* (KH, *Pt 2, Ch 11)*

According to our author, the hall-house was large so that, when Rognvald intercepts Thorfinn and Groa on their snowy way from Birsay to Orphir and purportedly seeks their hospitality at their destination, there is no problem in allowing that. However, en route Rognvald kidnaps Groa, he and Thorfinn fight and both men are injured. As a result, Thorfinn arrives at Orphir on a sledge and is surprised to see:

Stream and beach

... spread on the shore not only the buildings of his housestead, implanted between here and Swanbister, but six strange longships drawn up on the beach, and tents by the score set up on either side of the stream and halfway up the hill ... (KH, *Pt 2, Ch 7)*

The longships and tents on the beach and along the stream belong to Kalv Arnason, who has fled Norway.

Thorfinn and Groa are once more staying at Orphir when, some time after the sea battle off Hoy in which Rognvald was defeated and fled to Norway (see panel p. 36), another unexpected ship arrives on the beach. Groa's serving woman Sinna has put Erlend to bed and stepped out of her sleeping-hut.

> *... Then she saw a longship on the beach which had not been there at dusk.* (KH, *Pt 2, Ch 11)*

The longship is, of course, Rognvald's. He has come to murder Thorfinn by setting fire to the hall.

A gate in the kirkyard wall gives access to a path running alongside the stream down to the sea. It can be reasonably speculated that the badly burned Thorfinn carried Groa along here to the beach and the small boat in which they escaped to Caithness.

38 STROMNESS

The name of Orkney's second largest town (over 2,000 inhabitants!) derives from the Norse elements *nes* or headland and *straum*, which denotes the strong tides that swirl around the headland south of the town in Hoy Sound. Its alternative Viking age name was Hamnavoe – peaceful harbour or haven. Here we see the same Norse element *voe*, derived from the root word *vágr*, as at Kirkwall (see p. 8). At Kirkwall, *vágr* is translated to refer to a geographical feature (inlet or bay), rather than how it was used, as a harbour. For Hamnavoe, it was given the human-use translation. The town itself only dates from around the 16th century, but it has had two Norse names, so there was almost certainly a settlement there.

39 Bay of Skaill

> *[Thorfinn] seemed to take pleasure in Orkney in the wintertime, perhaps because of the winds that dragged through land and sea like a scraping-board and flung the green waves and white against the storm-beach at Skaill until the heathland was salt a mile inland ...* (KH, *Pt 2, Ch 13)*

Bay of Skaill

On the west coast, the Bay of Skaill bears the brunt of the strong prevailing westerly winds from the North Atlantic. It is the location of two of Orkney's most popular tourist attractions: Skara Brae, a Neolithic settlement older than most of Egypt's pyramids, and Skaill House, a 17th-century manor house.

D North Isles

40 Westray

Höfn ('haven', 'bay'), where Rognvald's main hall is situated, is now Pierowall ('small bay') on Westray. Both names derive from Old Norse. The island has Neolithic, Bronze Age, Iron Age, Norse (including a pagan cemetery) and later medieval historical remains. Though it is referred to many times in *King Hereafter*, no details are given. Rognvald sails there, his ancestral home, when he returns to Orkney for the first time since he left at ten years old.

> *... the three Norwegian ships sailed quietly north to the island of Westray, where stood the hall at Höfn, once the chief homestead of Brusi, Thorfinn's older half-brother and father to Rognvald.* (KH, *Pt 1, Ch 17)*

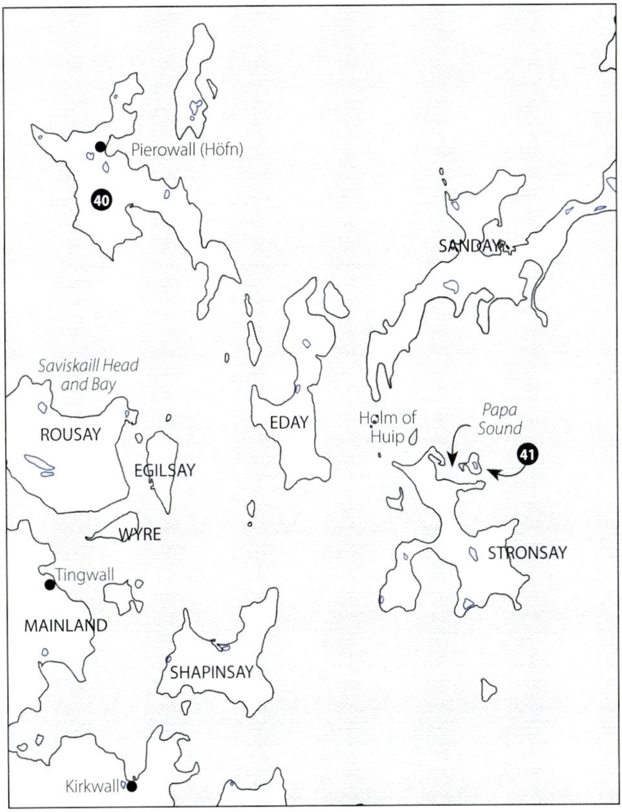

D NORTH ISLES
40 Westray
41 Papa Stronsay (Papay Minni)

And then, much later, after Thorfinn has had Rognvald thrashed following his interruption at the kingmaking,

> *[Rognvald says,] 'my lord King, you are welcome' ... There were forty men standing around him on the beach-head ... Behind Thorfinn on the jetty stood only Starkad his standard-bearer ...'* (KH, *Pt 2, Ch 4)*

Thorfinn has come to ask Rognvald to help deal with problems in Kintyre and Galloway. He has eight more ships off Saviskaill (*KH*, Pt 2 Ch 4, see map p. 33). Dorothy Dunnett does not specify that this meeting is at Höfn, but it is likely.

41 Papa Stronsay (Papay Minni)

> *... on Papay Minni ... the beach [of] streaked sand and boulders, with a few nousts built above the tide-mark, and above that, the strip-fields of the monks ... [the] soil ... was rich, and grew thick crops of bere, and some oats ...* (KH, *Pt 2, Ch 11)*

The ancient name for the island derives from 'Papar', a Norse-Gael word for 'Christian men' or 'monks' and indicates their presence here and on Papa Westray (Papey Meiri) when the Norse arrived.

Some months after burning the hall at Orphir, Rognvald goes, as usual, to Papay Minni to collect malt for Yule. Thorfinn sails in pursuit with Thorkel and his hird and, on arrival, has the monks' hall burned. Rognvald escapes and Thorkel follows him to the beach and kills him.

> *[Rognvald's men] rowed round Huip on Stronsay, and through Papa Sound, and into the monks' little jetty ...*
>
> *From north to south, Papay Minni measured less than a mile ... no man could hide on Papay Minni once night was over ...* (KH, *Pt 2, Ch 11)*

As indicated in the quote, this is one of the really small north isles. The remains of an 11th-century monastery may occupy the site of an earlier Pictish one and possibly this is the most northerly early Christian monastery known. The island is now owned by a traditionalist Roman Catholic order and is once again home to a monastery and farm. The monks are its only inhabitants.

Aerial photo of Papa Stronsay from the west

E Hoy

> *... Thorkel Fóstri had been talking of crossing to the mountains of Hoy, where the falcons were.* (KH, *Pt 4, Ch 14)*

'High island' is beautiful but rugged country. It figures most prominently in the sea battle between Thorfinn and Rognvald. Thorfinn is waiting at Thurso in Caithness (Loc 47). The approach of Rognvald's fleet from the north is signalled by a beacon on Hoy, which would have been located at the highest point at Ward Hill. Dorothy Dunnett sets the battle off Hoy's west coast (see panel p. 36).

42 Rora Head

Discussing the possible location of the coming sea battle between himself and Rognvald, and hoping to engage the enemy as far north as possible, Thorfinn says

> *'... [if we're unlucky] we shan't see much of him much of him till he's off Rora Head ...'* (KH, *Pt 2, Ch 10)*

They are lucky and the description of the battle puts it somewhere south of this promontory but still high up the west coast of Hoy away from the tumult of the Pentland

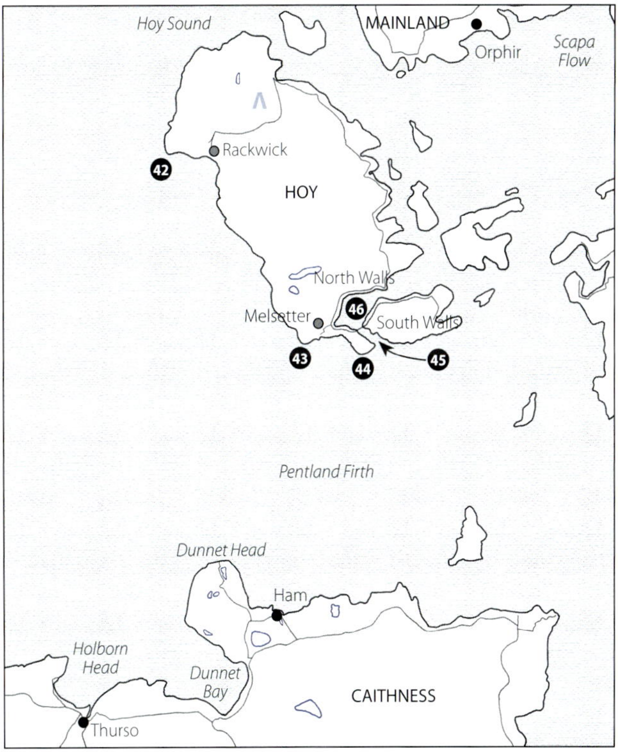

E HOY

42 Rora Head
43 Tor Ness
44 Brims Ness
45 Aith Hope (Aith Bay)
46 Longhope
Λ Ward Hill

The Sea Battle off Hoy (*KH*, Pt 2, Ch 10)

... as one Earl of Orkney set sail against another, the sea was the ally of neither and the potential enemy of both.

Thorfinn's fleet of sixty small ships and the larger *Grágás* are massed at Thurso in Caithness. King Magnus of Norway has both gifted Rognvald with ships and men and bribed Kalv Arnason to leave Thorfinn and support his enemy. Rognvald goes first to Westray with his Norwegian men before he and his fleet of thirty large ships sail south towards Caithness, as Thorfinn expects, through the North Isles and the along the west coast of Mainland and Hoy.

Based on the knowledge of weather, tides and currents, Thorfinn has calculated Rognvald's route and timing. When beacons signal that Rognvald is coming, Thorfinn's fleet puts to sea. A change in wind direction allows his ships to make good speed under sail and forces Rognvald's men to row. They intercept the enemy off Hoy. Thorfinn uses his more numerous ships to surround and overwhelm the larger vessels, supporting them where necessary with *Grágás*, a strategy which is initially successful. The battle continues with heavy losses on both sides until the wind drops and the tide drives the fleet, including Thorkel and Thorfinn who have the same enemy ship grappled, towards the cliffs. When Thorkel releases the grappling hooks the enemy crew leap overboard and have to be prevented from boarding Thorkel's longship. The Norwegian ship is then also freed from the grip of *Grágás* and it sweeps past Thorkel's. The tide is driving both ships towards the rocks. Thorkel loses control of his vessel and he and his men also jump overboard. Meanwhile, one of Rognvald's ships has now grappled *Grágás* and another approaches and starts to kill Thorkel's men in the water before turning its fire upon Thorfinn's ship. Thorkel and some of his men manage to get on board *Grágás* as it becomes clear that the group of three ships must separate and try to escape the flow carrying them towards the cliff. Then it is realised that, whilst the rest of both fleets are now rowing out of danger and the ships attacking them are disengaging to save themselves, a new ship is bearing down on them. It is Rognvald's flagship, and he is on a suicide mission to ensure Thorfinn's death. Just then, a mist descends and Thorfinn knows that he may have a means of escaping. The tide-race has taken hold of *Grágás*, and the remaining able men row the ship out of Rognvald's sight and away from the battle. *Grágás* successfully navigates two dangerous headlands on the south coast of Hoy to reach the bay in which the dead, and the skald Arnór, are put ashore and the ship is able to anchor. Thorfinn is able to reach Kalv, who, instead of joining Rognvald in the battle, has sailed his six ships from Westray to an anchorage on the east side of Hoy. Here, Thorfinn persuades Kalv to join his side and they sail back to the battle site as allies. As the fog lifts, the arrival of the fresh force proves to be the deciding factor. Rognvald engages *Grágás* and he and Thorfinn come face to face. Kalv grapples Rognvald's ship on the other side just as Thorfinn points out to his nephew that the Norwegians who make up the bulk of Rognvald's men are disengaging and sailing away. Although Rognvald turns to fight off Kalv, the men on his own ship refuse to obey his orders, cut themselves free of the enemy ships and join the rest of the fleet moving north.

Dorothy Dunnett's novelistic genius is seen to the full in her use of her single source for this incident. She incorporates all the elements outlined in the story told in the *Orkneyinga* saga into her brilliantly re-imagined and detailed version. Her beautifully realised battle scene describes the wind, weather and tide changes that affect the action, the criticality of the timing in these respects, and therefore the appropriate times of sailing. These are all hers. The circumstances of Rognvald's flight to Norway, of the resulting assistance of King Magnus and the sizes of his and Thorfinn's fleets are recorded in the saga, as is the break in the fighting, Thorfinn's recruitment of Kalv and Rognvald's subsequent defeat. Dunnett has woven her own theory of Thorfinn's intuition about what his nephew will do, and his planning to deal with it, into the bones of the saga's tale. She has also chosen to interpret the site of battle, perhaps for narrative purposes, differently from most scholars of the historical sources. This provides her with a logical place, not defined in the saga, to which Thorfinn can retreat in fog, meet Kalv and return to battle. Her location provides, in addition, a setting for exciting scenes of ships being forced onshore on the tide. It also allows her to have Thorfinn's fleet sail out from his home base on the coast of Caithness to heroically meet his foe.

The location, defined only as 'off Rauðabjörg' (red cliff) in the saga, is debated by scholars. For example, two translations give alternate possibilities, both in the Pentland Firth. One is on the north coast of Caithness, the other on the south coast of South Walls. Dunnett's choice of the red cliffs of western Hoy enables her to remain true to her historical source whilst providing her readers with a vivid description of the battle.

Old Man of Hoy from Rora Head

Firth. Rora Head is about a mile south of the sea stack known as the Old Man of Hoy, which can be seen from the Stromness–Scrabster ferry. On the footpath from Rackwick to view the Old Man of Hoy, Rora Head is on your left.

43 Tor Ness

The current and tide make this headland on the south-west corner of the island a formidable obstacle for Thorfinn's crippled and overloaded ship when escaping in the fog. Thorfinn says:

> *'When [the mist] gets to mast-height [the enemy will] disengage and start rowing. Otherwise the tide-race through the firth will simply swallow them. Look. It's catching us now. Whether we row or not, we're setting to the south of Hoy.'* (KH, *Pt 2, Ch 10)*

And Thorkel responds:

> *'White Christ, protect us ... Tor Ness is down there ... '*

The road does not reach the coast but it is possible to walk there from Melsetter.

44 Brims Ness

Having safely negotiated Tor Ness, this headland is another serious hazard to Thorfinn's ships.

Coastline near Brims Ness

> *[Their destination] was past the next headland, and the next headland at flood-tide was a killer ...*
>
> *A good man in a calm sea might circumnavigate Tor and Brims Ness by the kick of the eddy and the hiss of the breakers. Roaring down on the tide, lurching, juddering through the cross-currents, hammering into the fall-back, and squealing and grinding as her timbers and rigging complained,* Grágás *deadened the ear with her clamour ...* (KH, *Pt 2, Ch 10)*

Earlier in the story, Rognvald boasts of catching gerfalcons here. Attempting to provoke Thorfinn, he says,

> *'I was visiting Groa. I had found a pair of gerfalcons ... [at] Brims Ness ...'* (KH, *Pt 1, Ch 19)*

45 Aith Hope (Aith Bay)

> *The bay of Aith, a notch in the south coast of Hoy ...* (KH, *Pt 2, Ch 10)*

Escaping the sea battle he is losing, Thorfinn safely uses the fog to reach Aith Bay where he unloads the dead and wounded – and Arnór. Whilst here, the skald writes his verses about the battle he has witnessed.

Sitting on Aith Hope, where he had been forcibly placed with the dead and the wounded, Arnór had used his time well. (KH, *Pt 2, Ch 11)*

Dorothy Dunnett separates Aith Hope and Bay when they are, in fact, one and the same. Both are names for the water. Arnór's landing place might have been anywhere on the south coast of the bay.

46 Longhope

Longhope is a sea loch or bay on the south-east coast of Hoy. The name comes from the Old Norse. 'Hope' translates as bay as in Aith Hope (Loc 45) or, as here, as harbour or anchorage. The settlement of the same name on its south shore is, strictly speaking, located on South Walls, formerly a small tidal island now connected to Hoy by a causeway which carries the road. It is where Kalv Arnason awaits the outcome of the battle between Thorfinn and Rognvald.

... Arnór [had brought the news that] Kalv and his ships were not at Höfn with the rest of Rognvald's fleet, but had sailed south to Longhope, on the south-east of Hoy, for reasons ... easy to guess at. (KH, *Pt 2, Ch 10)*

Leaving his ship sheltering and anchored in Aith Bay, Thorfinn takes a skiff to visit Kalv at Longhope to persuade Groa's uncle to join him in resuming the battle with Rognvald. The causeway between the bays developed from two gravel spits which may, in Thorfinn's time, have allowed passage for a skiff. The longships probably travelled around South Walls to meet *Grágás* and sail back to the battle site.

North-East Scotland

Caithness and Moray still exist but the geographical areas of modern times are different from those of the 11th century. For simplicity, 'Caithness' and 'Moray' have been used here as Dorothy Dunnett used them in her story. The distribution of settlements in Caithness and the extensive area of north-east Scotland that formed the earldom settled on Thorfinn by his grandfather Malcolm II is, in lots of ways, the same as in the 11th century. None of the halls mentioned in *King Hereafter* have left their mark on the landscape, but it is surmised that many of the later now ruinous coastal castles were probably

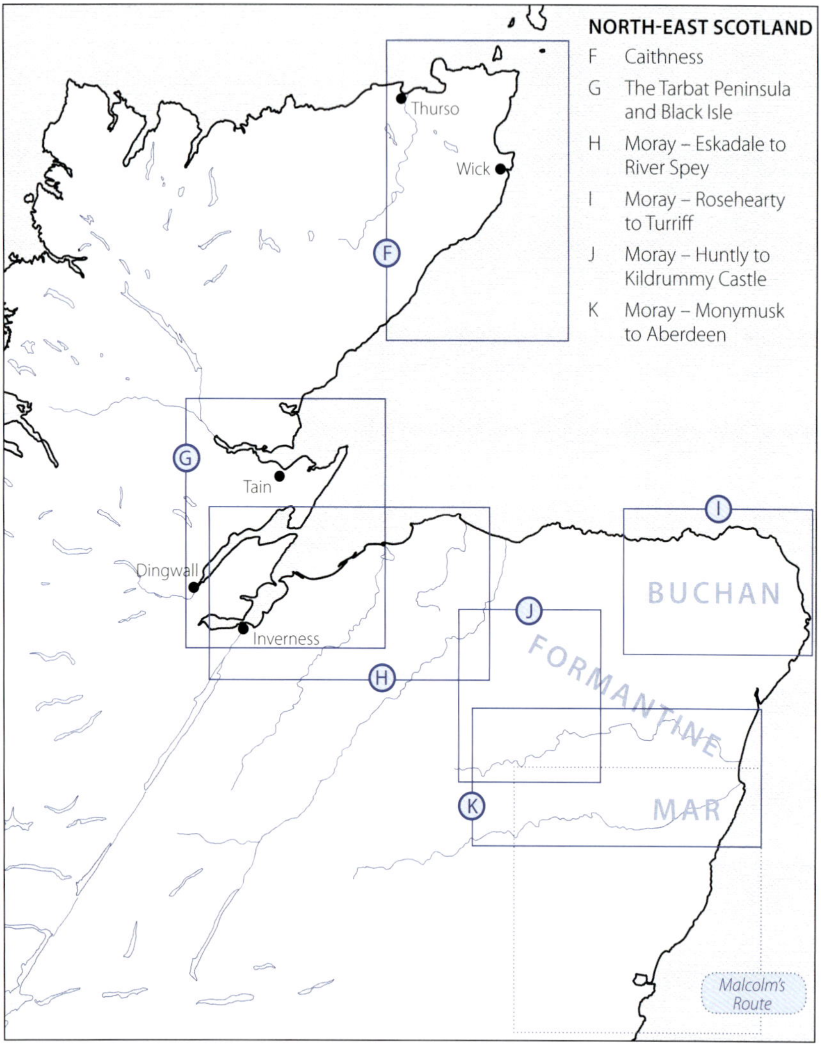

raised on the same sites as the Viking halls. Inverness, the only city of the area, is home to one quarter of the population. There are three sizable towns: Thurso, Wick and Dingwall. Tain is a large village. Most of the locations, particularly in the north, remain isolated settlements, hamlets or small villages numbering their inhabitants in family-sized units. The eastern areas of the region are mostly flat and, as intimated in *King Hereafter*, fertile farmland fills the coastal areas and wide river valleys (straths). As in Orkney, Dunnett journeys in this area are therefore largely about absorbing its atmosphere and exploring its wonderful coastline whilst getting a sense of the scale of Thorfinn's territories and taking advantage of the other historical and prehistoric sites in this beautiful country.

F Caithness

> *[Groa had visited Thurso and] also stayed briefly at Duncansby, at Freswick, and at Canisbay, where stood the most recent hall-house of all, on the high ground which looked down to the little thatched church of St Drostan's and the strand which ran along to the jetty at Huna. Two miles offshore lay the long green flank of the island of Stroma, with its snout pointing eastwards into the eddies.* (KH, *Pt 1, Ch 16)*

47 Thurso

> *The burned hall at Thurso had been rebuilt. In the event, Thorfinn had not taken her there, but to a new hall set on the heights overlooking the wide sweep of sands on the other side of the river.* (KH, *Pt 1, Ch 16)*

Thorfinn's fleet is frequently at Thurso and, on at least two occasions, his enemies are allowed to know or believe that he is there. Early in the story, having been warned by Sulien, Thorfinn's men are waiting for Gillacomghain's invading force. He is one of the brothers who had murdered Thorfinn's stepfather Findlaech.

> *[Thorkel and his men] had lain all day ... out of sight of the bay, and of the big timber hall, the collection of cabins and stockyards and barns, the one or two steadings that made up the settlement known as Thurso, on the rising ground between the beach and the river Skinandi.* (KH, *Pt 1, Ch 10)*

Gillacomghain's two-pronged plan, instigated by Crinan, to remove Thorfinn from Caithness results in Thorfinn being engaged in a sea battle off Deerness (Loc 13). Meanwhile, Gillacomghain marches on Thurso, which he finds apparently empty. He and his men enter the hall. Thorfinn's men, under Thorkel's command, move in and set fire to the hall killing all those inside. Dorothy Dunnett seems to locate this hall near to the beach, possibly in the area of the 11th-century Old St Peter's Church on Wilson Lane.

Another time, Thorfinn's dragon-ship returns to Thurso from a tax-collecting voyage to the Sudreyar (Hebrides) with Rognvald.

> *... her sails dropped. As she rowed her way into the rivermouth ... the larboard oars lifted as she slid to her berthing ... those [men] whose steadings were here, over the*

F CAITHNESS

47 Thurso
48 Holborn Head
49 Dunnet Bay
50 Dunnet Head
51 Ham
52 Reaster
53 Canisbay
54 Huna
55 Sannick Bay
56 Duncansby
57 Freswick Bay
58 Castle Sinclair Girnigoe
59 Wick
60 Helmsdale

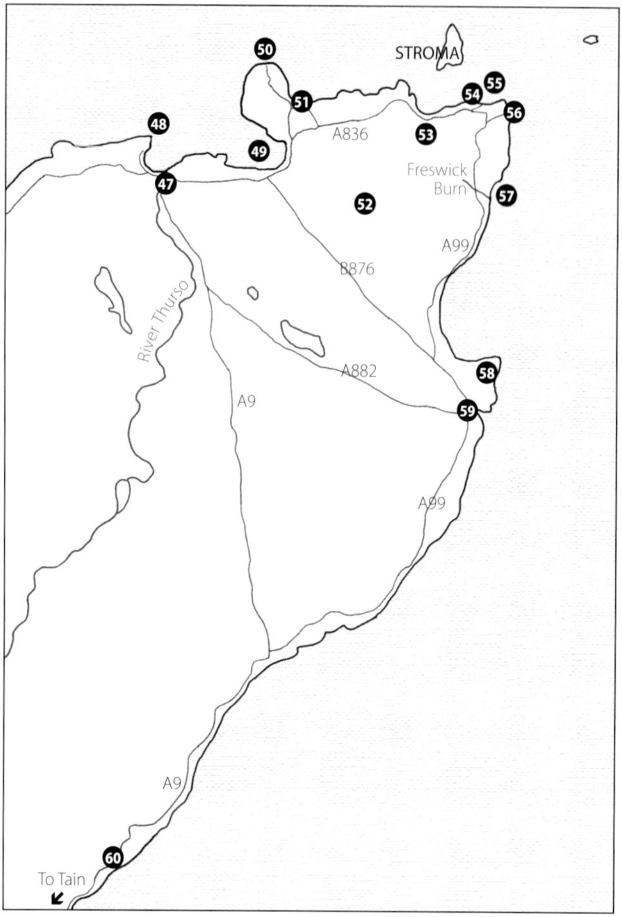

beach or along the riverside set off whistling for home; but the rest were already making their way to the hall ...(KH, *Pt 2, Ch 4)*

Larboard means port side, which implies that disembarkation is on the east bank of the river. There is no indication that the newly arrived hird have to cross the river to reach the hall, so on this occasion Groa is waiting for Thorfinn in the new hall on the rising ground in the east of the settlement. The Mount Pleasant area overlooks the river and the harbour, which occupies the old river mouth. It could be a location that fits the description. Both halls are, apparently, conjured out of Dorothy Dunnett's imagination because, although it is known that the Norse settlement mentioned in the *Orkneyinga* saga was centred on both sides of the river mouth, there is no evidence of any specific sites. The Thing's Va, an Iron Age broch overlooking the town from the south-west, is thought by some academics to be have been used as a *thing* site. Its name may be a corruption of the Norse *Þingvellir*, also the name of the important parliament site in Iceland. Its location between Tingwall in Orkney (Loc 18) and Dingwall in Ross (Loc 67) makes it an appropriate location for the governance of the north. It is the only possible Norse site to be identified in or around Thurso.

> As readers of *Iceland: The Dorothy Dunnett Guide* by Alyson JK Bailes will know, the pronunciation of Þjórsá, one of the rivers that the characters in *To Lie with Lions* have to negotiate as they return to their ship, is very similar to the name of this small Caithness town and river, especially when the local Scottish pronunciation, '*Thur-sa*', is taken into account. The name Dorothy Dunnett gives the river in the quote – *Skinandi* – means 'shining', and the word still exists in Icelandic.

48 Holborn Head

> *It was the beacon on Hoy ... that gave them their first warning, followed very soon after by the smoke from ... Holborn ... (*KH, *Pt 2, Ch 10)*

One of the beacons that warns Thorfinn of Rognvald's approach was on Holborn Head, the headland that forms the western arm of Thurso Bay, where the ferry terminal of Scrabster is located.

49 Dunnet Bay

> *Below the headland was the beach the fleet most often used and she took Lulach there, where, two miles long, the olive-brown wave-shadows moved in, one after the other, towards the unbroken sheen of the sand. (*KH, *Pt 2, Ch 4)*

The headland here is Dunnet Head (Loc 50), and this quote provides something of a conundrum. It is explicit that Dunnet Bay is a favoured beach, and yet it is never mentioned either by name or by implication except here. There are some instances when the description given to beaches at Thurso, some seven miles to the west, fit Dunnet Bay much better. The beach here is much longer than at Thurso, sheltered and perhaps most importantly, sandy. However, with rocks close to the shore, it would probably be usable only when the tide was right.

Dunnet Head

50 Dunnet Head

Alone in Caithness whilst Thorfinn is away trying to win back Rognvald's allegiance and friendship in the Western Isles, Groa is visiting settlements and areas of the north coast. She visits Dunnet Head, the tip of which is known as Easter Head.

Cliffs at Dunnet Head

> *Then she rode west to where the biggest headland of all stood dark red against the afternoon sky, and set her pony up round the lochans and bogs to the top, where she tied it to a rock and climbed to where the pony could not go but a man or a woman could lean on the wind as into the bosom of God and look upon the whole sunlit world of green grass and blue sea, from the land's edge that lay towards Norway to the smudged snow-capped peak of Ben Loyal, far to the west, pointing to the way her husband's ships had sailed ... (*KH, *Pt 2, Ch 4)*

The cliffs of the headland are of old red sandstone, and it is for this reason that Joseph Anderson, who edited a version of the saga published in 1873, speculates that the battle off Rauðabjörg (see panel p. 36) took place in this area. In the saga, Rognvald was sailing to Caithness to engage Thorfinn when he was intercepted in the Pentland Firth off Rauðabjörg.

It is unlikely that you will see Ben Loyal, which is some 60 miles west-south-west of Dunnet Head. But if the weather is clear, Stroma and Hoy will be visible across the Pentland Firth to the east and north, respectively, and you can watch the seabirds on the cliffs.

'... [A]ll the Dunnetts in the world come from Dunnet ...,' so said Dorothy Dunnett in a talk in the early 1980s.

51 Ham

Badly injured, Thorfinn is rowing from the burning hall at Orphir with a burned and miscarrying Groa towards the Caithness coast.

The bay at Ham

> *He knew where he was going, and he didn't need questions. ... 'We shall be safe long before dawn. I love you. Have I said so?' ... The family*

> *who lived in the turf hut on the rocks above Ham in Caithness were freed slaves ... [they saw] a boat there, far down on the mud, half in and half out of the tide-edge, and something moving, it seemed, at one end of it. (*KH*, Pt 2, Ch 11)*

In this atmospheric tiny bay there is a house and remains of a mill and millpond.

52 Reaster

When his presence at Ham is noticed, Thorfinn is told by Thorkel, '"I have found a place in Reaster for you ... Otkel my nephew is coming to Reaster and will work with you until you can hold a sword"' (*KH*, Pt 2 Ch 11).

Reaster, the site of a steading, is some six miles inland from Ham.

53 Canisbay

Canisbay is first mentioned as one of the many places that Groa and Thorfinn visit in Caithness.

> *... at Canisbay ... stood the most recent hall-house of all, on the high ground which looked down to the little thatched church of St Drostan's and the strand ... (*KH*, Pt 1, Ch 16)*

Thorkel is often there and Groa joins him when Thorfinn and Rognvald are away together and both she and Thorkel fear for Thorfinn's safety.

> *Groa could bear it no longer and, taking Lulach with her, set sail from the Tay to Caithness, where she joined Thorkel Fóstri at Canisbay ...*
>
> *From there she rode from one group of steadings to the next along the coast ... walked out ... to the shore. (*KH*, Pt 2, Ch 4)*

Canisbay Parish Church, the most northerly on the Scottish mainland, mostly dates from the 1600s and is a striking white building with a square tower on the A836 not far from the Gills Bay ferry terminal. As at Deer (Loc 78), St Drostan himself is reputed to have built a chapel in this area in the 6th century, and this church which is still dedicated to him stands on the site of a medieval church. From the kirkyard there is a fantastic view across the Pentland Firth to Orkney. The settlement of Canisbay itself is about half a mile inland, but the whereabouts of a hall is a matter of speculation.

54 Huna

> *They were repairing fish-nets at Huna, beside the grooved block of slate where the fish-hooks and the needles were rubbed, and the knives and swords, at a pinch, to keep them brilliant. At Huna, she stood with her back to a hurdle of dark trunks of seaweed and looked at the long dolphin shape of the island of Stroma, with white spray breaking and breaking under its neck, to the east. (*KH*, Pt 2, Ch 4)*

An atmospheric tiny harbour can be found at Huna. If the tide is right, there is a good chance that the beach will still be strewn with seaweed, as it is when Groa visits.

55 Sannick Bay

East toward Dunscanby, [Groa] stood on the broken, glittering shell-sand, white and liliac, of Sannick Bay ... (KH, *Pt 2, Ch 4)*

The white and lilac shell sand can be found in a small cove west of the main sandy beach.

White and lilac sand from Sannick Bay

... Thorkel Fóstri sailed ... to Sannick in Caithness, where Thorfinn had gone to settle a new dispute between Kalv Arnason's men and the old settlers. (KH, *Pt 2, Ch 9)*

Kalv had left Norway when he lost the reins of power in that country to King Magnus and sought refuge for himself and his hird with Thorfinn.

56 Duncansby

... the fulmars rose and fell with motionless wings in the salt airs round Duncansby Head ... (KH, *Pt 2, Ch 4)*

From the car park at the lighthouse on Duncansby Head you can take a footpath to view the sea stacks (and the fulmars and puffins). On the way is Duncansby Beach. Its usefulness to Thorfinn's longships in view of the cliff behind it is moot, but it is the only site that can be identified as a possibility. After Sulien overhears Crinan and Gillacomghain planning to usurp Thorfinn's earldom of Caithness, he sails north to warn his friend. He arrives at Duncansby.

Landing on the jetty at Duncansby, sending up to the steading to tell Earl Thorfinn that Sulien of Brittany and Llanbadarn was here ... Of course, the Earl had no idea he was coming ... [but it was] the same ... youth [who now] moved out of the steading ... and stood at a great distance, looking; and then ... covered the slope to the jetty in a matter of seconds ... (KH, *Pt 1, Ch 9)*

57 Freswick Bay

This year, [Thorkel] was at Freswick ... when Kalv's fleet moved in past the broch and round Skirza. Thorkel left the big steading and walked to the shore with the Havardson reeve to see the crews settled under canvas ... (KH, *Pt 1, Ch 3)*

Skirza and Freswick are scattered settlements on Freswick Bay and, though one is at the north and the other at the south end of the bay, they are accessed from the same road.

From the A99 take the road signposted 'Skirza 1.5 miles'. The first turning on the right is a track to the beach and Freswick Castle. The third turning, signposted 'Harbour', leads to the jetty and tiny harbour at Skirza.

> *[Kalv] stared out of the open door at the swept yard, and the river glittering in the sunshine, and the houses of Thorkel's kinsfolk and his serfs, and the farms that stood here and there over the bay, and at his own ship tied to its post on the sand, with the sea-edge like white tortoise-shell running layering in. It was a good bay, although open to the weather ...* (KH, *Pt 2, Ch 3)*

Kalv is at the steading with Thorkel. Freswick is known to have been the holding of Havard (Hallvardr), steward to Thorfinn's father, Earl Sigurd and, presumbly, father to Skeggi (Havardson).

The whole of the bay north of Freswick Castle, a privately owned tower house, is a well-excavated multi-period Norse site. The castle stands on the site of a 12th-century earl's longhouse, next to the beach by the Burn of Freswick with a hinterland of farmland. The location fits the quote exactly.

58 CASTLE SINCLAIR GIRNIGOE (RUINS OF)

Castle Sinclair dates to the early 17th century, but the earlier Castle Girnigoe was built by William Sinclair, 2nd Earl of Caithness, probably between 1476 and 1496. This William Sinclair was the older brother of Sir Oliver (Nowie) Sinclair of Roslin, friend of Nicholas de Fleury. Set on the cliff top on the southern arm of Sinclair Bay, this photogenic ruined castle has a spectacular setting whilst being only a short walk from the car park.

59 Wick

> *[Gillacomghain had dragged all their supplies and weapons of war all the way [to Thurso] from the east coast at Wick, where they had been landed ... [they] would have been moved to wonder, perhaps, at the empty house-steads at Wick and the lack of resistance ...* (KH, *Pt 1, Ch 10)*

Wick's name is from the Norse *vik* meaning bay. Early Norse jewellery was discovered in the 1800s. There is an archaeological site with a connection to St Drostan who founded the monastery at Deer (Loc 78). No more than a rectangular depression in the grass and known as the Chapel of St Tear at Ackergill, it is on the coast of Sinclair Bay about three miles north of the town and not far from Castle Sinclair Girnigoe (Loc 58). It may have been the site of a church founded by the saint. 'Tear' is thought to be a corruption of Deer, and the theory is that St Drostan may have landed here when sailing from his monastery in Buchan.

Wick itself is not at all prepossessing, but the coast is beautiful if the weather is fine. South of the town, and an easy walk along the cliff-top path is the small ruin of the Castle of Old Wick, one of the oldest in Scotland. It is thought to be have been built in the 12th century by Earl of Orkney and Caithness Harald Maddadson, possibly on an earlier Norse site.

60 Helmsdale

Helmsdale is one of the east-coast steadings used for storing supplies and receives some of the Moray ship-timber that Thorfinn fells (illegally) before Gillacomghain can stop him (*KH*, Pt 1, Ch 8). Later, after his injury at Loch Bracadale:

> *... Thorkel Fóstri did not like the new alliance [with Rognvald], nor what he heard of its subsequent course, from his sickbed at Helmsdale.* (KH, *Pt 1, Ch 18)*

Now a coastal village, the settlement at Helmsdale pre-dates the Norse invasion, although the present village was planned in the early 19th century to make provision for the influx of people made homeless by the Highland Clearances. Old Helmsdale is to the north of the village. This might point to the steading where Thorkel Fóstri recuperated, being situated somewhere along the river.

Next to the river on Lillieshall Street is the heritage centre *Timespan*. The centre also has a shop, bakery and café.

G The Tarbat Peninsula and Black Isle

61 Tarbatness

At the extremity of the northern arm of this hammerhead-shaped peninsula is Tarbatness itself. Today there is a lighthouse on the Ness and an opportunity for delightful walks from and around the car park.

The *Okneyinga* saga reports that Thorfinn the Mighty defeated the King of Alba in the Battle of Torfness. There are several theories about the site and who the participants were. Dorothy Dunnett's own research led her to the belief that it happened here and that Duncan was Thorfinn's Alban antagonist (see panel p. 50). Thorfinn prepares for battle in Dingwall (Loc 67), at the

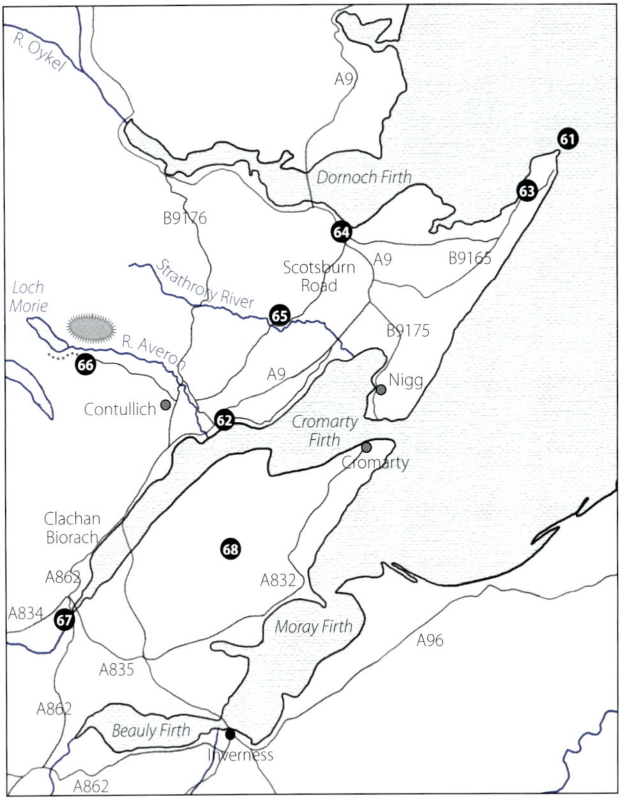

G THE TARBAT PENINSULA AND BLACK ISLE

61 Tarbatness
62 Rosskeen and Alness
63 Portmahomack (St Colman's/St Cormac's)
64 Tain
65 Scotsburn (Ulladule)
66 Boath (Glen of Thor's Goats)
67 Dingwall
68 Black Isle
Druim na Caerdaich

head of the Cromarty Firth, whilst sections of his army take up position in Tarbatness to trick his enemy and defend his back.

62 Rosskeen and Alness

Maldred, the leader of Duncan's ship-borne force, plans to land on the south coast of the Tarbat peninsula. The passage of his ship is the first to be described.

> *... his own landing place, at Rosskeen in the estuary ... one-third of the company ... northwards to Ulladule ... two-thirds ... [to sail up the firth] ... to land at a place called Clachan Biorach to attack Thorfinn's army from the rear.* (KH, *Pt 1, Ch 20)*

Thorfinn's agents on board ensure that his ship grounds on a sandbank. There is a phalanx of archers waiting on the beach, but it is not entirely clear where Dorothy Dunnett envisaged these events. They are led by Thorkel, who had left Dingwall (Loc 67) to ride 'to his command at Alness' (*KH*, Pt 1, Ch 20), which is nearby, so it might be either place. Rosskeen is in the middle of a two-mile-wide shallow bay, where, at low tide, the Rosskeen Burn can be seen trickling over the beach into the Cromarty Firth. The road runs next to the sea here but a small diversion, signposted to Achnagarron, to the board-

The Battle of Torfness (Tarbatness, *KH*, Pt 2, Chs 20 and 21)

Duncan brings his army north through Moray into Thorfinn's territory and arrives at the plain to the south of Dingwall, where Thorfinn and his men are waiting. Both antagonists plan to use the peninsula of Tarbatness to the north-east of Dingwall to support the main battle.

Duncan acquires three ships at Berwick in the south. They will land men at three different places on the peninsula to overcome the expected opposition, seize Groa and Duftah and, with that achieved, some men will re-embark and sail closer to Dingwall to support Duncan's land army. The rest will gather in Ulladule where they expect to find and defeat more Caithness men then march on Thorfinn's back. However, Thorfinn has enticed Duncan into his domain and has set traps for him in the peninsula. Duncan's ships were made conveniently available by Thorfinn agency, and Caithness men are aboard each one to sabotage the landings. Meanwhile Thorfinn's main force has moved into the peninsula. Some gather in Ulladule. Others go to the coast to successfully prevent the anticipated landings: one group to fire on an enemy ship which will be deliberately grounded on a sandbank, another to doctor the route through a bog and a third to engage Duncan's troops as they trek across a wide beach. Thus, it is men from Caithness who gather at Ulladule to support the rest of Thorfinn's army, not those from Alba. When they receive word, they move through the peninsula towards the fighting.

Meanwhile, the main battle begins when Duncan leads his army round the shoulder of the hill just south of Dingwall in the late morning to find Thorfinn waiting. By early afternoon, the Albans find themselves advancing in pursuit of an apparently retreating Caithness army. Duncan's troops become scattered as the fighting moves many miles to Ulladule, the valley of the Strathrory. He recognises he has been led into a trap when it is Thorfinn's men, not his own, that appear at his enemy's back. Duncan is defeated. He does not have his ships so he must escape westward through the hills where, he has been allowed to know, Groa and Duftah are sheltering. He finds them but his enemy arrives shortly afterwards. Thorfinn initially seeks to end the conflict by extracting promises from Duncan but is persuaded by Thorkel, who does not know that he is wounded, that he must fight his brother to the death. A single blow leaves Duncan severely injured and he is carried to his ships, which are allowed to sail south. Groa and Duftah return to the monks' settlement at St Colman's/St Cormac's and Thorfinn also makes his way there. Groa finds and cares for him when he succumbs to his injury. Whilst he is recovering, Thorkel brings news that Duncan's ship put into Forres and the king has died there. The kingdom of Alba is Thorfinn's for the taking.

ed-up church just beyond the railway bridge where it is possible to park, gives an opportunity to identify the whereabouts of the burn, even when it cannot be seen from the main road. There is a pedestrian bridge over the stream between the railway bridge and the road. This watercourse is, however, very small and the term 'estuary' in the quote im-

plies that these events do, in fact, take place at Alness (about two miles to the west) at the mouth of the River Averon. This sandy area, and the extraordinary beauty of the Cromarty Firth on a fine day, can be viewed from Yankee Pier, a remnant of World War I, which can be accessed from a path that runs alongside the Dalmore Distillery on the B817.

With Maldred's men overcome, the ship is taken over by Skeggi's men. It is not able, therefore, to move on to its designated destination of Clachan Biorach. This possibly Neolithic feature, which may have been a stone circle or a chambered cairn, was destroyed in the 19th century. The site is a cultivated knoll on the side of a hill about halfway between where the Cromarty Bridge carries the A9 over the firth and Dingwall (Loc 67).

63 Portmahomack (St Colman's/St Cormac's)

> *... Dubhdaleithe ... was allowed to ... [leave] his abbey of Deer, to settle with a group of disciples on a piece of ground by St Cormac's chapel on the shores of the Dornoch Firth ... (*KH, *Pt 1, Ch 19)*

St Colman's is now known as Portmahomack, a transliteration of its Gaelic name, which translates as *Haven of St Cormac*. Cormac and Colman are both translations of the same name. Dorothy Dunnett uses both. This attractive village, three miles from the Ness, has the unusual attribute of being an east-coast village facing west. It was a major Pictish site, subsequently used by the Celtic church and, in our author's imagination, a Norse settlement. It is a landing site for Duncan's invading army and the place where Groa and Thorfinn recognise their love for one another.

Thorfinn sends Groa to stay with Dubhdaleithe (Duftah) who has moved here from Deer (Loc 78) until, with Duncan's attack imminent, they and the monks take refuge at the glen in the hills (Loc 66). A little later some of Duncan's troops arrive.

> *The knörr sailed as close as it could ... Muiredach's men jumped into the sea, dividing into sections ... for there was a palisaded fort on the high ground above the sand and the rocks ... The fort ... was deserted, and the little church held nothing ... One small party ... made its way to the east to scour the land between St Colman's and the point at Tarbatness. The rest ... turned west through the bogs and marshes ... (*KH, *Pt 1, Ch 20)*

Nothing remains of the fort, but an area of bog and marsh lies to the west and there

is a pretty beach. A church still sits on highest point. The village moved to the harbour from the area between the church and beach in the 1940s, and the building known as Tarbat Old Church was left on its outskirts. Now it is the Tarbat Discovery Centre, a museum that records its Norse connections but is chiefly devoted to the presence here of a major Pictish religious community. A succession of churches has occupied this site since the 6th or 7th century. In the 11th century the church was part of a monastery, and the chapel belonging to Duftah's community is undoubtedly one that stood on this site. Indeed, part of this building was extant in Duftah's time, as it retains a portion of the 8th-century crypt.

Following Thorfinn's single-combat fight with Duncan (Loc 66), Groa returns to the monastery.

> *... [She] travelled back with the monks to St Cormac's. ... arrived at last by the chapel, and waited only to learn that the bundles containing her gear had been left outside the empty houses she and her household had used. Then ... she set off alone to find herself a cabin.* (KH, *Pt 1, Ch 21)*

She finds Thorfinn alone and severely injured. It is while she is nursing him that they make a discovery.

> *'Is it compassion?' 'No' ... 'I am beginning to wonder if we may not have something greater ... Is that what you wanted to say?'* (KH, *Pt 1, Ch 21)*

The centre can be visited free from Easter to October but opening hours vary.

64 Tain

This (now) town also features in the manoeuvring before the last battle between Thorfinn and Duncan.

> *[One of Duncan's ships] rounded the point at Tarbatness, passed ... St Colman's ... towards Westray ... [but, due to sabotage of the steering oar and sails] arrived at her appointed landing-place when the sun had already risen and the tide had receded ... [so] that the river Tain ran out to the firth over a stretch of pink sand that seemed to stretch shoreward to infinity ... they disembarked on the flat sand and had marched halfway across it before they saw ... the armed forces drawn up ahead of them.* (KH, *Pt 1, Ch 20)*

Ruined chapel at the St Duthus Burial Ground

Tain was probably an early Norse settlement. *Baile Dubhthaich*, its Gaelic name, means 'Duthac's or Duthus's town' (the names are interchangeable). He is the town's patron saint and there are references everywhere. Three ecclesiastical sites were dedicated to him and are part of the *Tain through Time* visitor experience, which begins at the museum in the High Street. A 13th-century chapel became a place of pilgrimage and sanctuary after his remains were interred there. Now a picturesque ruin, the St Duthus Old Burial Ground is on Chapel Road, near the golf course. The open land next to the nearby public car park gives good views of the estuary of the river where the attempted landing took place. On Castle Brae is the now deconsecrated St Duthac Collegiate Church, to which the saint's relics were moved and enshrined when it was built in the 14th century and in its grounds are the ruins of the old parish church also dating to the 14th/15th century.

Readers of *King Hereafter* know the saint as Duftah; indeed, Groa reports that Lulach calls him St Duthac. His dates are usually given as 1000–1065, and Dorothy Dunnett believed that he was born in Tain. There is, though, little certainty about anything about him. In *King Hereafter*, Duftah is high-born, possibly of a Norse-Gael dynasty, and his active role in the story ends when he leaves to become Abbot of Armagh.

It has not been possible to identify why Dorothy Dunnett refers to Tain as Westray. The only other occurrences of the name are in Orkney where the Norse name translates as West Island. Duftah's monks are described as the 'community of St Cormac by Tain' (*KH*, Pt 1, Ch 19), even though Portmahomack and Tain are 10 miles apart, implying that Tain was the larger, more well-known location.

65 Scotsburn (Ulladule)

> *... [Thorfinn's] three troops ... raced to join one another in the gentle green heart of Ulladule, with its church and farmhouse, where the Strathrory river left its glen and wound down to the firth mouth.* (KH, *Pt 1, Ch 20)*

This wide valley in the centre of the Tarbat peninsula plays a major rôle in the events of the battle which ends in Duncan's death. The Albans plan to muster there, but it is used instead by the men of Caithness, who gain ascendancy in the bloody skirmishes across the peninsula.

The Strathrory River runs in a glen north of and parallel to the valley until it turns south-eastward as it emerges to cross Ulladule at today's settlement of Scotsburn. From here it changes its name to Balnagown as it flows on into the Cromarty Firth.

The Scotsburn Road that runs through the area is an attractive one which gives a feel of the landscape. En route to or from Tain, it crosses high ground affording spectacular views of the Cromarty Firth, with its row of unemployed or retired oil rigs. The road is unnamed on paper maps, but is off the A9 south-east of Tain. From Ulladule, any of the signposted roads lead back to major roads with the route to/from Alness being the most likely line of Duncan's advance from Dingwall (Loc 67). The Strathrory glen can be viewed from outside Ulladule from the Strathrory Bridge on the B9176.

66 Boath (Glen of Thor's Goats)

Groa and Duftah wait out the battle at a farm and smithy overlooking the River Averon, which runs from Loch Morie to the sea near Alness (Loc 62). It is where Thorfinn finally confronts and mortally wounds his half-brother.

> *... Groa... left the little huts she shared with the people from the farm and the smith's house below, beyond the bogs of the river ... the cattle [were in] the hills beyond the loch ... From the edge of the little hill, she looked into the blackness, east and south ... and wondered what the morning would bring.* (KH, *Pt 1, Ch 20)*

Duncan realises that he has lost the battle and is escaping westward when he learns of Groa's whereabouts at 'the Glen of Thor's goats ... where the River Averon ran down past the smith's house' and calculates that it is '... not so far from Strathrory. Four miles or five ...' (*KH*, Pt 1, Ch 21). Later in the same chapter, the point of view moves to Groa's location. We learn that '... there was a long view from the Druim na Caerdaich.' A child sees Duncan approaching from the other side of the river from this ridge of higher ground. It is about six or seven miles as the crow flies from Ulladule (Loc 65, longer by road) and not far from the loch, near an area called Boath. Dunnett imagined Groa's refuge here in the hills of Ross because Duncan was reputedly killed at a place associated with a smithy, and Boath translates from Gaelic as 'smith's booth'. It is reached on a single-lane track with passing places through an estate managed for hunting, fishing and forestry. Boath is signposted on the B9176 at Contullich. At Boath, the track forks and narrows still further (see a sign for Glaik Croft on the left and farm buildings on the right) where there is a parking place. The roads straight ahead and to the right make a mile-long loop which comes close to the river about 400 yards further on. Depending on how recently the trees have been harvested, the circular walk is more or less attractive, but the view of and walk alongside the River Averon is well worth the effort, especially if the sun is sparkling off the water. The north bank climbs

River Averon at Boath

View of Dingwall and Ben Wyvis from the Black Isle

steeply up to the high wooded ridge of Druim na Caerdaich. Aware now of the river valley and the ridge running parallel to the road, the drive back towards the B9176 is captivating and very evocative. It is easy to imagine Dorothy Dunnett's characters here, and to understand why our author loved it herself.

67 Dingwall

Although the only mention of Dingwall in *King Hereafter* is in connection with the battle which ended with Duncan's death, this rather unremarkable town was a very important site in the 11th century. It was a major *thing* site, and many sources describe the hall reputedly rebuilt by Thorfinn after the battle as 'magnificent'. Sadly, the town makes nothing of this history and the satisfaction here is in the search more than in the quality of the finds.

Duncan's army is marching north to engage Thorfinn and the men of Orkney and Caithness. Thorfinn has plotted to entice Duncan out of the lands over which the king of Alba has dominion and into his own territory of Ross.

> *... the stance would be made further north, at Dingwall ... There [Thorfinn] had the big hall and the Moot Hill by the mouth of the River Peffer, where the long sea inlet reached into the hills. To gain the Tarbatness peninsula, a marching army would have to pass between the sea and the mountains of Easter Ross, where Dingwall, the assembly place, lay.* (KH, *Pt 1, Ch 20)*

As the two armies begin the battle, the northmen shout:

> 'Thorfinn! Thorfinn!' *The hoarse double syllable ran from hill to hill and up to the peak of Ben Wyvis.* (KH, *Pt 1, Ch 20)*

This must have been very loud, as the thousand-metre summit of Ben Wyvis is about seven or eight miles north-west of the town.

Dingwall's river, the Peffery (Peffer) flowed into the sea at the head of the Cromarty Firth, and the Norse settlement grew up as a port on the south side of the estuary. As a result of silt deposition, the town is now separated from the sea by a mile or so of mud-flats and sandbanks.

The head of the early medieval estuary is thought to have been approximately at St Peter's bridge on Tulloch Street near Peffery Park. The river has been canalised since the 18th century, and a canalside path, signposted from St Peter's Bridge, leads to an area where you can, depending on the tide, see mudflats or the sea. Archaeologists have found evidence that Old River Road just north of the bridge follows the line of the left (north) bank of a swampy estuary. The positions of the moot hill and castle probably give a general idea of where the right (south) bank was.

MOOT HILL

Historian Barbara Crawford suggests that, whilst the town has a Gaelic name, *Inbhir Pheofharain* meaning 'the mouth of the Peffery' (which is still acknowledged in signs around the town), the preferential survival of Dingwall's Old Norse name – *Þingvöllr*, 'parliament field' – indicates that this function was of major importance. At the southern extremity of the Norse earldom, Dingwall is ideally situated for use as a *thing* site.

South of Dingwall [Duncan's] army woke at dawn ... They marched round the hill-shoulder and down to the Moot Hill. (KH, *Pt 1, Ch 20*)

The main road from the south still skirts the hill. Though the moot hill is not immediately obvious, it has, in part, survived. Indeed, it is in the middle of a municipal car park off Tulloch Street in the centre of the town, and in view of the Tesco's car park.

The mound is popularly referred to as Moot Hill, which is the term also used by Dorothy Dunnett but which is a later, feudal, term not in use in the 11th century. The term's etymology is debatable, but it is roughly synonymous with *thing* and a 21st-century archaeological dig established that the mound, on which an obelisk known as the Cromartie Monument stands, is definitely the moot hill/*thing* site of the Norse era, although it was much reduced in size in the 20th century.

A dig revealed that the mound was raised in the 11th century, possibly over a prehistoric feature. The archaeologists

Site of the Moot Hill

Dingwall Castle Doocot

speculate that Thorfinn may have built it after the Battle of Torfness (Tarbatness, Loc 61 and panel p. 50). There was a large surrounding ditch which probably touched the then-shoreline. There are indications that the site may have had links with a church on the same site as the present St Clement's on Church Street near the car park entrance. The petrol station next to St Clement's occupies the site of the field on which participants in the *thing* would gather and the Gallows Hill area on the western fringe of the town was associated with the justice element of a *thing*.

THE CASTLE (POSSIBLE SITE OF THORFINN'S HALL)

Dingwall's royal castle is recorded in the 13th century. It was almost certainly built on the same site as Thorfinn's hall, close to the river estuary and the *thing* site. It remained in royal hands until the late 16th century. The castle fell out of use and its ruins have now been almost entirely replaced with modern buildings. Stones from the castle were reused to build a dovecote in the early 16th century, and it is the only publicly viewable fragment that remains. Dingwall Castle Doocot is on the edge of a property on the residential Castle Street. There is no information board or any other indication of its history and the names of the roads here are the only commemoration of the site of the castle, and by extrapolation, of Thorfinn's hall.

DINGWALL MUSEUM

The museum housed in the former Town House (council office) is run by volunteers and opens for the summer. The central part of the building was originally the late 18th-century tolbooth.

68 Black Isle

The Black Isle is the most southerly territory on the east coast within Thorfinn's domain and offers a huge view back to the head of the Cromarty Firth and Ben Wyvis can be clearly seen above and behind Dingwall (Loc 67).

None of the action in *King Hereafter* is set in the area, but Gillacomghain, as Mormaer of Moray, takes advantage of Thorfinn's absence at Canute's court to invade his territory and Thorkel does battle with him on Thorfinn's behalf.

> *... it took a week of fighting to clear Gillacomghain and his men out of the Black Isle and back to the south side of the Moray Firth.* (KH, *Pt 1, Ch 7)*

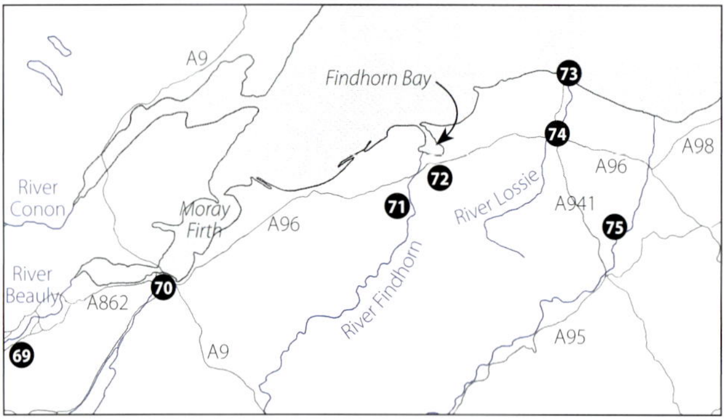

H MORAY – Eskadale to River Spey

69 Eskadale
70 Inverness
71 Darnaway (Tarnaway) Castle
72 Forres
73 Lossiemouth (Kineddar)
74 Elgin
75 River Spey

Today this peninsula has picturesque villages, sea-life watching, gentle countryside walks and the Cromarty–Nigg car ferry which, with a capacity of four cars, must be one of the smallest anywhere. It is an area not to be missed.

Moray

In *King Hereafter*, Gaelic-speaking Moray encompasses territory from the Moray Firth in the north to the River Dee, where Aberdeen now stands, in the south. It probably extended westward through the mountains to the west coast. East of Inverness and the narrows where the River Ness enters the sea, the inner part of the firth is known as Beauly Firth and the River Beauly reaches the sea at its head.

H Moray – Eskadale to River Spey

69 Eskadale

This is a very small area deep in the Highlands, approximately 16 miles from Inverness, where the Eskadale Burn flows north-west into the River Beauly. It is a settlement of a few houses.

Duncan is planning the forthcoming action against Thorfinn:

> *Eskadale, on the next firth, was undefended ... Thorfinn was coming down ... from the north ... but not in time to save the Cromarty peninsula.* (KH, *Pt 1, Ch 20)*

The 'Cromarty peninsula' is the Black Isle. The reader knows, as Duncan does not, that Thorfinn has deliberately stayed further north, as he explains to Thorkel:

> *'Once he steps beyond Eskadale, he is in my land with an invading army and must face the consequences.'* (KH, *Pt 1, Ch 19)*

It is not clear why Eskadale is the border of Thorfinn's territory, since the River Beauly is much bigger. Perhaps the border ran from the north-east to the south-west, as shown on some maps of Norse Caithness, or Dorothy Dunnett is using it to denote a much more

The River Ness, looking north from the 19th-century castle

broadly defined area. Duncan approaches the northern border of Moray near to the coast. His scouts tell him that Eskadale is undefended – so he continues to march north.

70 Inverness

The city of Inverness stands at the head of the Great Glen, a geological fault running diagonally across the country, which provides a natural coast-to-coast land route through the mountains and which would have been of great strategic importance. It is likely, though unprovable, that control of Inverness and the Glen was a major point of contention between the Orkney earls and the mormaers of Moray. Certainly, the ancient region of Ross to the north, which in the book is part of Thorfinn's earldom, was once part of Moray. Although the location is not mentioned until much later, the story begins with Thorfinn arriving in Norway to petition the king after he has escaped the hall fire that killed his stepfather. We later learn where that happened when he is lying injured after his own burning by Rognvald at Orphir. Thorkel Fóstri visits him and asks:

> *'... at Inverness ... Was that how you escaped?' ... Thorfinn [replies] 'Findlaech showed me. But he was too heavy for the loft-floor.' (*KH, *Pt 2, Ch 11)*

Thorfinn becomes Mormaer of Moray after the death of Gillacomghain. Some three years later he arrives, unannounced, to visit his wife at Inverness where Groa is in dispute with a trader. Her slave Sinna is ready, if necessary, to give a signal to archers to fire on the trader and,

> *... [Groa] was sitting placidly under her awning on the wharfside ... [with] the Mormaer's hill directly behind her ... [when] Sinna ... flung her arms to the skies ... her kerchief ... still in her hand. Dutifully, the row of spearmen and archers on the Mormaer's mound released their weapons ... [to rain] steadily, with no very beneficial effect, on a dragon-ship bearing the black-raven banner of Orkney. (*KH, *Pt 1, Ch 13)*

The site of the wharf cannot be identified, but Dorothy Dunnett said that the mound from which Groa's men fired on Thorfinn is the hill where the modern residential roads Auldcastle Rd and Victoria Terrace now stand. Nowadays it is about a mile from the coast and river estuary and about half a mile to the north-east of Inverness Castle, which is a 19th-century iteration of a fortification and stands on one of two ancient sites next to the river. The site was first used by Malcolm III, who reputedly burned down Macbeth's 'castle' and built his own here.

About 300 yards north of the castle, the Old High Church stands on another mound overlooking the river where it is known that an early Celtic church stood. Beside the shore, in South Kessock, there is a park with carparking and picnic tables at Merkinch Local Nature Reserve where the mouth of the river can be viewed.

71 Darnaway (Tarnaway) Castle

In *Gemini*, Nicholas and Nowie Sinclair take Jodi salmon fishing in the Findhorn.

> *'Have you ever fished off Darnaway Castle? I assure you, it is an experience fit for angels.'* (Gem, *Pt 3, Ch 32)*

So says Nowie Sinclair to Nicholas when persuading him to stay in the north after the visit to Orkney. There has been a castle in the forest at Darnaway since the early 14th century. Today's mansion dates to 1810 but retains the timber roof of the banqueting hall built in 1450, part of the baronial castle set in royal hunting forest close to the River Findhorn. It is the private residence of the Earl of Moray, but the hall is sometimes open by appointment during the annual Moray Open Doors weekends in September.

72 Forres

Forres, whose name is probably Gaelic, is important to Thorfinn. It is where he takes oaths of fealty from the men of Moray, where he marries Groa, where Lulach's son is baptised and where, after his losses at Dunsinane, he learns of the changes in Europe and Normandy that will ultimately end his life.

Thorkel arrives from Norway the day before Thorfinn will marry Groa.

Beach at Findhorn

> *As the wind ... let his ship sweep under sail towards the white stretches of sand that marked the mouth of the river Findhorn, he saw lying inland not only the blustered smoke of the wood-and-wattle settlements he remembered, but the gleam of new timber ringing the fortified hill of Forres beyond it, and within that, a long thatched roof he did not recognise, above which blew a flock of bright and unfamiliar banners. At the mouth of the river, there was a new building among the fishermen's huts, from which a couple of men put off in a skiff and, boarding, steered the helmsman round the skeined sandy course of the river. Below the hill, the old jetty at the crossing was already manned, and at its far end they could see a scattered party of men moving downhill from the stockade towards them.* (KH, *Pt 1, Ch 11)*

Today, the River Findhorn opens into a large bay which narrows where it meets the sea. The Burn of Mosset, a small tributary of the Findhorn which drains into the bay, runs through the town of Forres, which is situated a mile or so south of the confluence. The white beaches of the quote can be accessed from Findhorn. The original harbour and fishing village were washed away in the 17th century when the bay was formed.

Duncan makes rendezvous here with the three ships he will use to do battle with Thorfinn at Tarbatness (Loc 61 and panel p. 50).

> *At Forres, as Duncan had expected, the folk from the rath [ringfort] settlement and the river had all taken their beasts and locked themselves behind the palisades of the hall-mound. (*KH, *Pt 1, Ch 20)*

It is said that a royal 'castle' existed in Forres from the 9th century. The source for this information is not clear, but there is a mound at the west end of the High Street called Castlehill Gardens which Dorothy Dunnett confirmed was the site she had in mind for the timber palace. The term *rath* (ringfort) implies that she imagined that there were associated buildings inside fortifications on the mound.

This was a Pictish area of settlement, as indicated by the 9th-century seven-metre-tall cross-slab called the Sueno Stone. Its complex carvings are uniquely fine, and it still stands in the area in which it was originally erected. It would have overlooked the marshy ground between the Findhorn and the Mosset and now stands, enclosed in glass, near the A96 road in the north-east of the town.

73 Lossiemouth (Kineddar)

Towards the end of *King Hereafter*, Tuathal returns from Bremen where he has been consecrated as bishop.

> *[He] found [Groa] with the household at Kineddar, by the sand-strewn flats of the Lossie ... (*KH, *Pt 4, Ch 14)*

Lossiemouth has been developed west of the river mouth since harbours were built in the 18th century. It has fine beaches, and Kineddar is commemorated in the name of a street near the marina. Archaeological sites on the B9135 immediately south of the junction with Coulardbank Road show that the settlement itself was situated south-west of today's town centre and confirm a Christian settlement dating back to Pictish times. Many of the finds made here are now in the Elgin Museum.

74 Elgin

Elgin is six miles to the south and an attractive town. At the end of part 1 of *King Hereafter*, the blow Duncan receives from Thorfinn after the battle at Dingwall (Loc 67) proves mortal. He dies after being put ashore from the ship taking him to Berwick to be cared for by the monks near Elgin, possibly the ones at Kineddar. Many historical sources claim that the final battle between Macbeth and Duncan took place near Elgin and that Duncan died at Bothnagowan (meaning 'smithy'), now called Pitgaveny, about two miles north-west of the town.

75 River Spey

Thorfinn is preparing for an invasion by Gillacomghain.

> *For ships, for shelter, for defences, they would need wood ... the best and straightest trees ... were in Moray, and the rolling spates of the Spey would bring them riding out on their rafts to the sea.* (KH, *Pt 1, Ch 8)*

Spey Bay was, for two centuries until the early 20th, a major shipbuilding area using timber rafted down from the forests in its hinterland just as Thorfinn does. In the 15th century, it was important for both timber and fishing, as attested by Tam Cochrane in *Gemini*.

> *'[The Sinclairs] are strong on Speyside ... with the fishing and timber ...'* (Gem, *Pt 1, Ch 4)*

Pitsligo Bay

There is a riverside walk at Boat o'Brig on the B9103 north of the A95.

I Moray – Rosehearty to Turriff

The 11th-century mormaerdom of Moray included the ancient region of Buchan, which is in the far north-east corner of today's Aberdeenshire. There are three locations here, one where Groa first meets Abbot Dubhdaleithe in *King Hereafter* and two from *The Ringed Castle*.

Lymond, his men and the Russian ambassador are shipwrecked here near the end of their voyage from Arctic Muscovy. In the historical record their landfall was in Pettislego and the survivors were given hospitality by the local lairds. Dorothy Dunnett has used this information in her story. The single underwater archaeological search was unable to confirm the site of the wreck named in the historical record as Pettislego but Dorothy Dunnett chose the bay at Rosehearty.

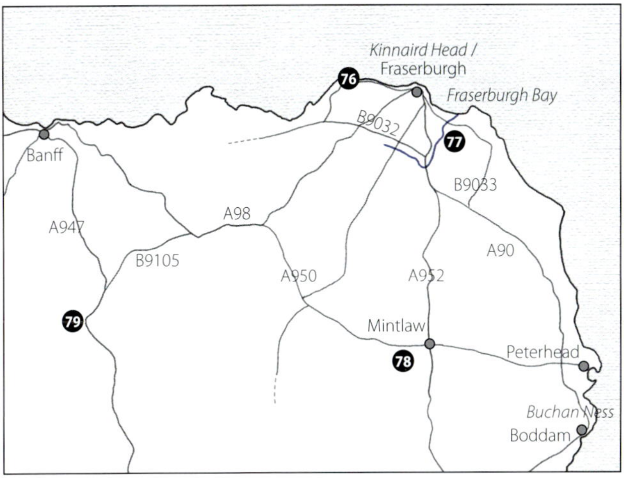

I MORAY –
Rosehearty to Turriff

76 Rosehearty (Pitsligo Bay and Castle)
77 Cairnbulg Castle (Philorth Castle) and Water of Philorth
78 Old Deer (the monastery at Deer)
79 Turriff

The first sight of land for the voyagers is Kinnaird Head. The headland is now an open space in Fraserburgh and the site of the Museum of Scottish Lighthouses, housed in the former Fraserburgh castle. The town was founded by the Frasers of Philorth in the second half of the 16th century presumably using the riches afforded by the shipwreck. The Forbes family of Pitsligo similarly were able to enlarge both their castle and the nearby settlement of Rosehearty.

76 Rosehearty (Pitsligo Bay and Castle)

Having passed Kinnaird Head

> *… on November 10th [1556] … Chancellor … sailed slowly up to the broad, rocky coastline … and felt his way into the nearest small bay which gave promise of shelter … They had time, before the light went, to see the outline of a fair-sized keep on the skyline … reefs behind and beside them … (*RC*, Pt 3, Ch 2)*

Some hours later, the wind changes, the ship is driven onto the reefs and only a few survivors make it to the beach in the

> *… pretty bay, half-moon in shape, with white grainy sand rising to thick sweet grass, still very green. Below were the slabby rocks, sloping down to the sea … (*RC*, Pt 3, Ch 2)*

The survivors gather around a bonfire and

> *… they said … Sir Alexander was coming; and somebody else. He supposed they were the local lairds, one of them belonging perhaps to the castle he could see … (*RC*, Pt 3, Ch 2)*

The 'local lairds' were Sir Alexander Fraser of Philorth and John Forbes of Pitsligo

whose castle is an attractive and fairly extensive ruin today. Although only about 300 yards from the sea and on rising ground, it cannot now be seen from the coast road. (The nearby Pittulie Castle, which can be seen from the road, dates from the turn of 17th century.)

> *... they had been swept into the tall keep of Pitsligo ...* (RC, *Pt 3, Ch 3)*

The square keep seen from the *Edward Bonaventure* was built by the Frasers in the 15th century but passed by marriage to the Forbes family shortly after. The great hall was the setting for the judicial enquiry ordered by Mary de Guise into the ship's lost cargo, of which the lairds of both Pitsligo and Philorth denied all knowledge. The original tower house can still be discerned amidst the ruins of what became a substantial castle with a courtyard in the years after the shipwreck. Pitsligo Castle is maintained by a trust whose sole trustee is still a Forbes.

77 Cairnbulg Castle (Philorth Castle) and Water of Philorth

> *... the ampler hospitality of the manor of Philorth ... What was left of the cargo of the Edward Bonaventure was transferring itself, swiftly and effectively into the pockets of Buchan, and Alec Fraser seventh Laird of Philorth, four miles to the south-west of Pitsligo ... was doing little to stop it.* (RC, *Pt 3, Ch 3)*

When, on the second morning after the storm, Richard Crawford arrives at Philorth he sees

> *the forty-foot grey castle of Philorth, with its new keep and round tower rising from its green mound, and the white running light of its stream, spilling through the short marshy grass to the dunes and between the rocks to be lost in the sea ...* (RC, *Pt 3, Ch 3)*

The stream that Richard notices is the Water of Philorth, which still flows across the

Water of Philorth

beach to reach the sea. On this coast the sea has been receding for centuries, and when the castle was first built in the 14th century, and probably still in 1556, it was at the estuary of the Water of Philorth at the south-east corner of Fraserburgh Bay. Despite Dorothy Dunnett's inclusion of them in her description, the dunes did not develop until the 20th century.

> *[Richard] saw, far off, a man standing ... [and] set out towards him ... [now] resting in a coign of dun and grey rock ... Lymond did not move ... You cannot embrace a seated man whose ... hands ... remain strictly clasped round his knees ... (*RC, *Pt 3, Ch 3)*

The catastrophic meeting confirms all Lymond suspects about his birth and sets Richard once more in opposition to his brother.

The beach can be reached by following the brown sign 'Water of Philorth' on the road B9033 near the entrance drive to the castle. The keep and round tower are still part of the castle but, now surrounded by trees, cannot be seen from the road or beach. It was abandoned by the Frasers in favour of their new castle at Kinnaird Head but, now known as Cairnbulg, it is once more the home of the senior branch of the family in the person of the daughter of the Chief of the name and arms of Fraser and visits can only be made by appointment by writing to The Hon. Mrs Nicholson, Cairnbulg Castle, Fraserburgh, AB43 8TN.

About twenty miles south of Fraserburgh is Buchan Ness and its lighthouse. Signposted to Boddam on the A90 it is almost the most easterly point of mainland Scotland and is mentioned in the plotting which culminates in the sea battle off Deerness (see panel p. 15) and the death of Gillacomghain. Crinan explains that half the fleet will be sent

> *'... straight north from Buchan Ness [so] that [Thorfinn] can have no warning until it is too late.'* (KH, *Pt 1, Ch 9)*

78 Old Deer (the monastery at Deer)

The marriage ceremony of Thorfinn and Groa at Forres (Loc 72) is conducted by the Prior of St Drostan's of Deer using

> *... the altar-silver and vestments which Deer already owed to the generosity of Findlaech's family ...* (KH, *Pt 1, Ch 11)*

Earlier, the monastery had become Sulien's place of learning when his intervention to foil the plot between Crinan and Gillacomghain to drive Thorfinn from Caithness changed his own plan to study in Ireland. Discussing the matter with her son and the Abbot of Llanbadarn Godiva asserts that

> *... Earl Thorfinn has arranged for him to study at St Drostan's instead ...* (KH, *Pt 1, Ch 9)*

Archaeology points to an organised 10th-century presence and according to legend the community was founded by the saint himself in the 6th century. As one of the centres visited by the couple when Thorfinn is establishing his right to the mormaerdom of Moray it was one of the places

> *... where the monks had come first, long ago, and where most often there remained a small monastery or a collection of huts round a chapel dedicated to one of the familiar saints.* (KH, *Pt 1, Ch 11)*

Deer is also significant for Thorfinn and Groa because it is the home of the

> *... hearty-spoken man with a beard called Dubhdaleithe, whom Groa fell into conversation with because he was Abbott [sic] of Deer ... (*KH*, Pt 1, Ch 15)*

Indeed, it is at Deer that Duftah and Sulien care for and tutor Lulach.

The monastery was abandoned for a new Cistercian monastery in the early 13th century and it is the ruins of Deer Abbey that can now be visited. The archaeological dig in 2018 revealed what appear to be the long-lost buildings of Duftah's monastery in a nearby field to the west of the ruins.

The Abbey survived until the Reformation and the site is now in the care of Historic Environment Scotland. The ruins are well signposted, well worth a visit and free. The entrance is on the A950, north-west of the village of Old Deer.

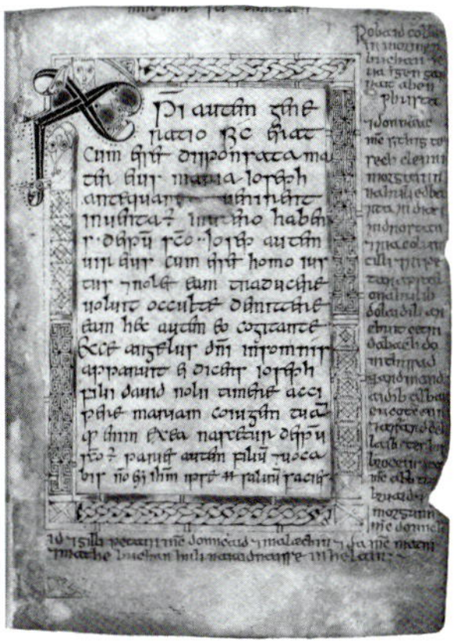

THE BOOK OF DEER

Now at Cambridge University Library, the Book of Deer is thought to be the oldest surviving Scottish illuminated manuscript. It dates from the 10th century and is a small pocket gospel book written in Latin by a single hand with later marginalia in the earliest known examples of Scottish Gaelic. These notes describe the foundation of the original monastery by St Columba and St Drostan and make reference to landholdings which led to the archaeological dig. Scholars believe the book was made in Scotland even though it is similar to Irish gospels. Perhaps it was written at Deer by Irish monks!

79 Turriff

> *Groa, moving from Turriff to Deeside with her five-year-old son and her household, was overtaken and stopped by a fast-riding group of men led by Skeggi, whom she knew but did not approve of. With no preamble, he instructed the Lady of Moray to turn round her troop and accompany him forthwith ... (*KH*, Pt 1, Ch 19)*

Duncan is moving north to engage in battle with Thorfinn, and Groa is prevented from journeying into danger and taken to safety at Tain (Loc 64).

In Turriff, Groa would have stayed in the Columban monastery which had been established in the previous century. No trace remains of the monastery, but the earliest church is thought to have existed in the 7th century on the site of St Congan's Old Church, the ruins of which can be found behind buildings on Putachie Path (Castle Hill, near Tesco Superstore). Malcolm III reputedly built a church on this site after his defeat of Macbeth. If true, perhaps the monastery was in this vicinity. The present ruins are from the 15th and 16th centuries.

J MORAY – Huntly to Kildrummy Castle

80 Huntly
81 Rhynie (Essie and Noth)
82 Cabrach
83 Tap o'Noth Hill Fort
84 Dufftown (Mortlach)
85 Auchindoun
86 Kildrummy Castle

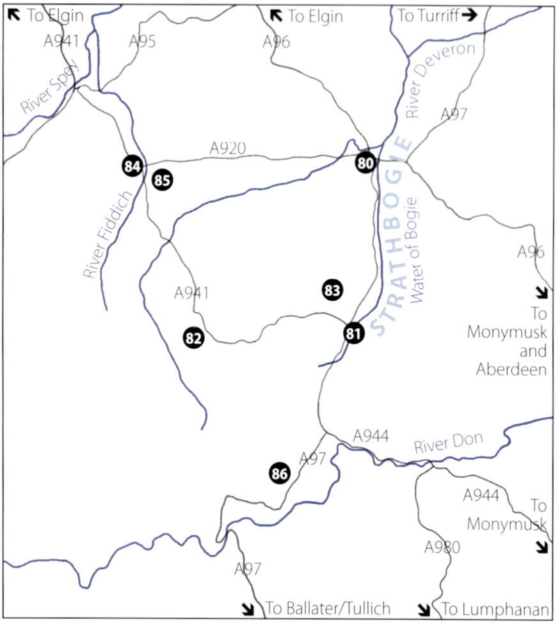

J Moray – Huntly to Kildrummy Castle

80 Huntly

When Thorfinn tells Groa that Coulter (Loc 90), on the southern border of the mormaerdom, will be her dower lands, it is observed that they are

> *... also the wardlands that protected the north-driving pass of Strathbogie: the route an army from Forres might take if it wished to march south without trusting the coast and its shipping. The route an army from the south of the same mind might use if it wished to invade Mar and Moray.* (KH, *Pt 1, Ch 11)*

Duncan does precisely that when he moves north towards Dingwall (Loc 67).

> *The Irishmen [in his army] talked; and Duncan, marching up the Vale of Strathbogie, heard them, and was no longer disturbed.* (KH, *Pt 1, Ch 20)*

For most of its length, the Water of Bogie flows through the wide and shallow Strathbogie from south of Rhynie (Loc 81) north to Huntly and its confluence with the River Deveron. The A97 road runs through the historically strategic pass. The small town of Huntly, itself previously known as Strathbogie, boasts a ruined castle similarly known in the past by both names.

81 Rhynie (Essie and Noth)

In the period of recuperation after the battle at Dunsinane

> *Thorfinn was staying at … his little hall at Noth, beside Essie.* (KH, *Pt 4, Ch 12)*

This is also where historians believe Lulach was killed by Malcolm III less than a year after Macbeth's death.

> *Lulach … kissed him and said, 'I have nine months, I told you.'* (KH, *Pt 4, Ch 20)*

Essie is a district containing one small hamlet in the parish of Rhynie and Essie.

Noth Parish Church is in Rhynie, and 'Noth' is part of the names of several farmsteads and abandoned cottages on the A97 north of Rhynie.

82 Cabrach

> *… [Thorfinn came] back from his ride through the hill-pass between Spey and Don, with a smell of snow in the air from the Cabrach.* (KH, *Pt 4, Ch 12)*

This is an area of about 10 by 8 miles of mountainous land and dramatic scenery at 300 metres above sea level. It is one of the most remote areas in Scotland. Cabrach has a small and falling population which still speaks Doric, the dialect of Scottish particular to the north-east.

The area is also visited by Nicholas and Jodi in *Gemini*.

> *They climbed over the Buck of the Cabroch [sic] while they were travelling …* (Gem, *Pt 3, Ch 33)*

This 700-metre cone-shaped peak can be seen from the A941 at the junction with the road signposted to Lumsden.

Buck Mountain, Cabrach

Tap O'Noth Hill Fort

83 TAP O'NOTH HILL FORT

This 600-metre mountain is the site of an extensive hill fort complex of 800 huts now thought to date from the 3rd century BC and on into the Pictish period. It can be reached by a path from a car park on the A941 west of Rhynie. With a possible population of 4,000 at its height in Pictish times, it may be the largest known settlement in post-Roman Europe. The many stone circles and cairns in the area are testament to continuous human occupation over millennia.

84 Dufftown (Mortlach)

Mortlach Kirk

> *Latterly [Thorfinn] had spent a week or two here in the mountains, dividing his time between Mortlach and his little hall at Noth.* (KH, *Pt 4, Ch 12)*

The site of Mortlach, the settlement near the River Spey that Thorfinn visits from Noth, is on the southern edge of Dufftown, deep in the Grampian mountains. It is an area of ancient habitation as testified by Pictish remains and evidence that they were evangalised in the days of St Columba by St Moluag, who founded one of the oldest churches in Scotland here. The present church, which retains some 13th-century features, notably the chancel which probably outlines the simple rectangle of the early church, stands on the same site that Thorfinn would have known. The area around the church is one of the few specific places that we can be reasonably sure Thorfinn visited. When he is gravely ill immediately after the Dunsinane battle, Groa knows that this is one of the settlements he can be moved to if necessary.

> *... Deer and Mortlach, whose doors stood open to receive him if danger returned.* (KH, *Pt 4, Ch 10)*

A plaque on the graveyard wall commemorates a victory of King Malcolm II over 'Danes' in 1010. Modern scholarship suggests the sources actually refer to the battle nearby in which Malcolm III defeated Lulach, but it is an interesting connection to *King Hereafter*.

Dufftown describes itself as the Malt Whisky Capital of Scotland and there are nine distilleries in the town using locally grown barley. In the north of the town, the ruins of Balvenie Castle are open to the public.

85 Auchindoun

During their trip to the north (in *Gemini*, Pt 3, Ch 33) Nicholas and Jodi, with Tam Cochrane, 'scrambled all over Auchindoun'. The ruins of the L-shaped 15th-century castle is signposted on the A941 about 2 miles east of Dufftown.

86 Kildrummy Castle

The extensive ruins of this 13th-century castle are magnificently set at the top of a steep slope and guarded by a deep ditch on one side. It was the seat of the Earls of Mar. It is visited by Nicholas, Jodi and Tam Cochrane in *Gemini*.

> *... [they] rode south to Kildrummy. Master Cochrane was Constable of Kildrummy Castle.* (Gem, *Pt 3, Ch 33)*

K Moray – Monymusk to Aberdeen

87 Monymusk

> *Monymusk had been Lulach's choice, and she thought Thorfinn would have approved it. Its little stone church and the hall and hospice and cabins on the banks of the Don stood buttressed by the low hills of Mar, safely north of the borders of Angus, whose loyalty was as yet unknown ....* (KH, *Pt 4, Ch 10)*

After the battle at Dunsinane, Monymusk provides a relatively nearby refuge for the severely injured Thorfinn.

The church in Monymusk dates back to the 12th century. It served the Culdees of the nearby monastery and stands on the site of an earlier church, so it is almost certainly the church referred to in the quote. A 9th-century intricately carved Pictish cross-slab can be found inside. As was common, the Culdee community was small, possibly around 12 priests. Later the community was refounded as an Augustinian priory. In the 16th centu-

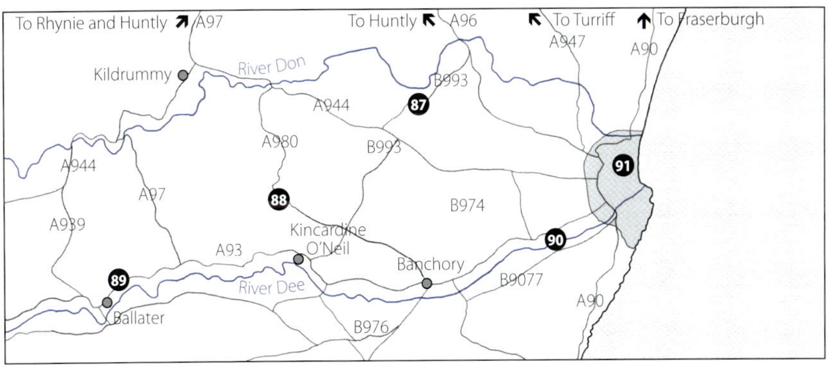

K MORAY – Monymusk to Aberdeen

87 Monymusk
88 Lumphanan
89 Tullich
90 Coulter (Maryculter, Peterculter)
91 Aberdeen

ry, the run-down buildings and facilities were acquired by the Forbes family, who used the stonework left over from earlier looting to build a castle on the monastery site. Now known as House of Monymusk and still a private residence, it sits on the bank of the River Don about 300 yards behind the church. There is parking space behind the village hall next to the church and the driveway to the house begins just over the bridge by the cemetery.

Monymusk Parish Church

88 Lumphanan

The village name derives from 'Church of St Finan' in Gaelic and it boasts the Macbeth Arms pub, a tea shop and a general store, as well as an ex-church dedicated to the saint. Groa chooses to go to Lumphanan for the birth of Thorfinn's first child, Sigurd/Paul, whilst her husband waits at a nearby hill fort, possibly at Mortlich Hill, about four miles away.

> *... Lumphanan, set in wooded hills between Monymusk and the Dee river ... Surrounded by pools and by marshland, the rising ground by the small church was safe, and held within its stockade all she required in the way of buildings to serve herself and her household ... [she felt better] walking about the well-kept timber buildings on the higher ground, and down and over the causeway to the houses of the people who lived here all the year round ...* (KH, *Pt 1, Ch 14)*

Whilst the church is not named here, the high-status buildings around it imply a monastery, and even though the nearest attested Culdee house was at Clova (Kildrummy, Loc 86), more than 10 miles away, archaeology on the site of the current building revealed evidence that it was an ecclesiastical site between the 7th and 13th centuries.

The site is more clearly identified at the end of the book when Thorfinn arranges to meet Groa at Lumphanan where he will make his last stand against Malcolm.

> *'I will see you at St Finnian's hill at Lumphanan.'* (KH, *Pt 4, Ch 15)*

The stone building that was the church cannot be visited as it is part of a cluster of buildings which makes up a private home on the south-west outskirts of the village. It can best be seen on the high ground to the north side of the unnamed road from the village to the Peel Ring (see p. 73). However, the fact that it sits on a separate small hill can only be appreciated from a much closer viewpoint on another unnamed lane off the road to the Ring. There, between the entrance to the house and the Burn of Lumphanan flowing under the road, the hillock can clearly be seen.

Peel Ring

Lumphanan is where the story ends, but even though the battle of Lumphanan is semi-historical, there is no certitude about its location. There are four sites around the village associated with legends of Macbeth's death, the first (see box below) being on the same lane as the ex-church. There is a trail beginning near the pub.

MACBETH'S WELL

Local legend says Macbeth drank at this well before the battle. The remains of the stone wall around a well can be glimpsed on the same lane as the church (Loc 88) a few yards from the burn.

PEEL RING (POSSIBLE SITE OF THE BATTLE OF LUMPHANAN)

The Ring, an atmospheric site in the care of Historic Environment Scotland, is free to visit and has a carpark. Locally it is described as the site of the battle of Lumphanan between Macbeth and Malcolm, but it is now known to have been raised in the 13th century as a short-lived timber castle and re-occupied in the late 15th century by a stone house whose foundations can still be discerned. The cluster of buildings on higher ground to the northeast of the mound contains the church of St Finan.

Macbeth's Well

MACBETH'S STONE (PLACE OF MACBETH'S DEATH)

This natural stone, the legendary place of Macbeth's beheading is a very short walk from the Ring. A gate gives access across the field to the small rise on which it stands. It is certainly not Dorothy Dunnett's 'flat plot of ground' (*KH*, Pt 4, Ch 15) where the novel's final duel takes place.

MACBETH'S CAIRN

Macbeth's body was supposedly laid, briefly, to rest at this Neolithic cairn ruin near the road out of the village to the north-west, behind the Howburn farmstead.

89 Tullich

On their post-marriage tour of Thorfinn's new mormaerdom, Thorfinn and Groa reach the River Dee. The boggy ground forces them to use a barge, probably, though it is not entirely clear, upstream from Coulter (Loc 90). By the Tullich Burn, they make their last stop.

> *... [they] drew in where the boards had been laid at the mouth of the stream ... five ways met at or near Tullich, including the pass that led north to the Don, and so it was a brisk little hamlet, with room for market-booths at the Dee crossing, and storage barns, and a good, well-built house for the toisech ... The next morning, as the sun rose behind Cullblean [sic] ... [a messenger] ... rode into Tullich ... (*KH*, Pt 1, Ch 12)*

Tullich was once the most important settlement on upper Deeside. It was a thriving community until the growth in Victorian times of the village of Ballater which is about two miles to the west. This is a fertile area where the valley of the River Dee widens, close to the mouth of the Tullich Burn which flows into the Dee from the north through the Tullich Glen, with the hill called Culblean on its eastern flank. There is archaeological evidence of buildings, including longhouses, immediately west of the burn behind the farm called Milton of Tullich.

The only visible remnant of the settlement at Tullich is the roofless early 15th-century church which can be found next to the A93 Ballater Road. Tullich Kirk stands to the east of the burn on the site of a 7th-century Pictish church dedicated to St Nathalan. A number of Pictish stones are displayed in the kirkyard and it has been postulated that this concentration of stones may indicate the existence of a relatively large and important ecclesiastical community, a theory supported by radiocarbon dating in the churchyard which indicates the presence of a monastery from the mid 7th to late 9th centuries. The history of the church is recorded

Tullich Kirk

Malcolm's Line of March from Alba into Moray

Dorothy Dunnett outlines the route Malcolm and Tostig take from Alba to the last meeting at Lumphanan. Although King Duncan's march to his losing battle with Thorfinn began at Perth and Dunkeld and was longer, continuing as it did via the Vale of Strathbogie to Forres and on to Dingwall, his journey through the mountains may well have been the same as his son's. Malcolm leaves Glamis for Forfar and Brechin in Alba before using a pass through the Mounth to reach the river Dee 'between Banchory and Kincardine' (Kincardine O'Neil today). This is most probably the route of the Old Military Road (B974) via Fettercairn and Bridge of Dye which, once over the summit, branches to the west to become an unnamed road signposted to Finzean. At the T-junction at Whitestone, after a few yards eastbound on the B976, the road continues north once more to Potarch, which is 'something like two miles or perhaps three from Lumphanan' (*KH*, Pt 4, Ch 15).

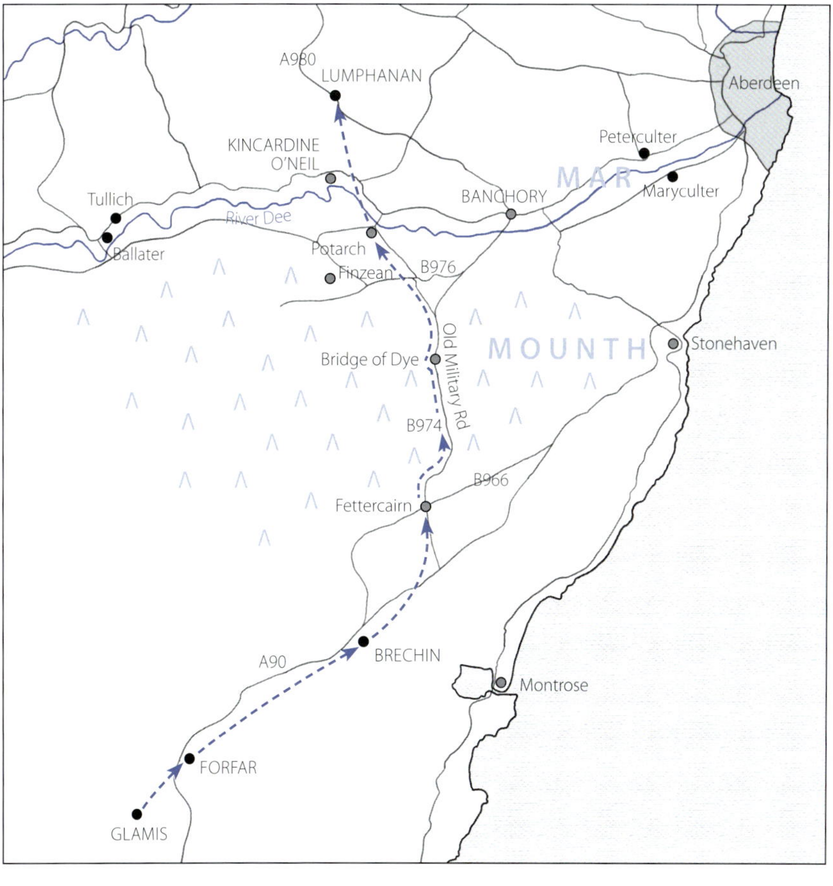

more fully on information boards at the site.

90 Coulter (Maryculter, Peterculter)

> *'... I shall give you the lands of Coulter on both sides of the Dee to hold for your son as your morgen-gifu ...'* (KH, *Pt 1, Ch 11)*

So says Thorfinn to Groa on the morning after their marriage. In *Gemini* it is noted that the Knights of St John hold the salmon rights at Peterculter (*Gem*, Pt 1, Ch 10).

Groa's dower lands are now two villages, one on each side of the River Dee. Maryculter (or Kirkton of Maryculter) is a village south of the river and Peterculter to the north is, administratively, a suburb of the city.

91 Aberdeen

> *... they moved on ... to Formartine ... And for their last visits of all, they made their way along the frontier of Mar, where the river Dee rolled down through its broad heathlands from the hills where lay Coulter, the bride's dower lands.* (KH, *Pt 1, Ch 12)*

Formartine is only mentioned as one of the places that Thorfinn and Groa visit in the early days of his kingship. There are no obvious historical remains of an important settlement, and the name has only survived as a local administration area, the name of a football team and that of a long-distance walk. It seems to have stretched from the River Don at Aberdeen north-west towards Huntly. Groa and Thorfinn's specific destination cannot be identified. Immediately to its south and on the southern border of Moray was the historical province of Mar. Mar was a narrow strip of land about 9 miles wide which stretched from the coast into the mountains, centred on the River Dee and immediately north of the formidable barrier of mountains between Moray and the kingdom of Alba.

Aberdeen has no known Norse connections, but the bishopric is mentioned often in *Gemini* and John le Grant is from there. When leaving the north, '[Jodi] travelled to Aberdeen with his father, and got a place on a boat going to Leith' (*Gem*, Pt 3, Ch 33).

Old Aberdeen dates from the 15th century. There is a wonderful 16th-century church dedicated to St Machar.

Here, we reach the southern extent of the territory held by Thorfinn before he becomes King of Alba. Look out for the forthcoming guides, which will include *Scotland: Central Lowlands* and *Scotland: the West Marches*. These will include all of the Alban and Cumbrian locations from *King Hereafter* as well as those from The Lymond Chronicles and The House of Niccolò.

ORCADIAN PRONUNCIATION

broch – 'ch' as in Scottish 'loch'
brough – 'ough' as in Scottish 'och' in 'loch' (i.e., same pronunciation as broch)
Dingieshowe – Ding ees how ee
Einar – ayn-uh
Harray, Sanday, Stronsay – the 'ay' ending in all place names ending is pronounced 'y'/'ee' so Harry, Sandy, Stronsy (and signs for the 'Real Harray Potter' to be seen all over the West Mainland!)
noust – noost
Orphir – Orfer
Rognvald – Ronald

A NOTE ON THE MAPS

Mainland is sometimes given the Latin name 'Pomona/Pomonia' on maps. It is not used by Orcadians and arises from an early 16th-century mistranslation of Roman author Solinus. *(from: Orkneyjar.com)*

Acknowledgements

Particular thanks for assistance with the text of this guide are extended to Anne Artymiuk, Dr Ragnhild Ljosland, Patricia Long and Anne Mitchell in Orkney; the Timespan Heritage Centre, Helmsdale; Debbie Joy of the Lumphanan Heritage Society; Jonquil Nicholl; Sam Llewellyn; Sidney Foubister of Verona Boat Tours at Skaill; and my colleagues Deborah Conway Read, Deirdre McCormack, Heather Schlusemeyer, Julie Trail, Nicky Cannon, Heather Jacobson and Suzanne McNeill. Their help is much appreciated but any errors that remain are my own.

The Dorothy Dunnett Society also thanks Penguin Books for permitting us to reproduce the quotations from the novels.

Members of the Dorothy Dunnett Society are currently creating a Wiki that includes information on *King Hereafter*:

https://dunnettcentral.org/wiki

Some elements are there already – type in 'Thorfinn' and see what comes up.

15
16
17
Pinthland firth
The Swell
The Heppers
Stroma
The boyer
Dunesbe hea
Hoborne head
Quinicnap head
Brynesy ness
Halladayle flu.
Strathy flu.
Strathy head
Torsuthy
Hyp Iland
Shyp Iland
Ilen Martyn
Ardquhytyn
Conne Ilen
Hory
Herreford
Ardurnes flu
Colne
Drudon
Tounge ca.
Glenik
Tew
Comak
Far
Strathy
Halladail
Dimay
Fors
Strbubaster C.
Thurso
Dunnet
Olryk
Braul
L.Vrdall
Far flu
L.Naver
L.Rulsid
L.Glas
L. Caldel
Caithn
Fors flu
Wattin
Spittel
Bowar
Fresick cast
Keis
Arckyrgyll cast
Girnega C.
Catnes
Weik
Latherne
Fors
Old Weik
Ness head
Dunbeith Cast
Maydenpapes
Baridale flu
Helinsdale
Baridaile cast
The Ord head
Browra
Clyne flu
Stranavern
Laxford
Foilles
Strath
Leith
L. Shyn
Forsnar
Wissle flu
Clyne flu
Kyldon
Iners bin
Braywhart
Done flu
Cliniter illa
The marble
mountaines of
Sutherland
Felag
Rogart
Clyne
Culmaly
Dunrobin cast
SUTHER LAND
Ferne
Scelbo
Shynfl
Pal Rossin
Onis flu
Dorno
Tarbartness
Cassaw flu
Cillan flu
Strath
Carron flu
Tournogarg
Tayn
Claigan
Tarbart
Balnogavi cast
Tayne
Kean ca.
Carron
Foulis cast
Fern
Nyg
Cromarty flu
Hills of Allabaster
of Rosse
Cromarty
Chanonry
Dingwall
Rosse
Rosermark
Red cast
Bewly Abb.
Kair
Ardmanoth
Lein
Louet cast
Tray
Vrquhart
cast
Lochnes
Moyn
Glennen
Vrquhart
Invernes
Nesse flu
Petty
Ranive
Marden fl.
Kylrac cast
Ardyrseir
Tornway cast
Forres
Plus carty ab.
Calder cast
Soilles
Moyr
Kenny
Bean cast
Tala
Findorne flu
MURAY
Thalen flu
Spey flu
Strath Spey
Bullyk flu
Airn flu
Cast
Carry
Kingusy
Ellan Moy
La Garve
The Lake of Nessa never freseth
Grampius Mountain
Lossy flu and Spine
Spey flu
Innes
L.
C.Spyn
Killos ab
Elgin
Boggich
Rothes cast
Bevany
ca
Anchindlen
cast
Bruntkirk
Vale of Speu
Clait
Strathdo
Glentoner
Taver flu
Kindrok
Kingka
Muralho
Pinth
Sker
Sow.
Dunesbe hea
Fynla

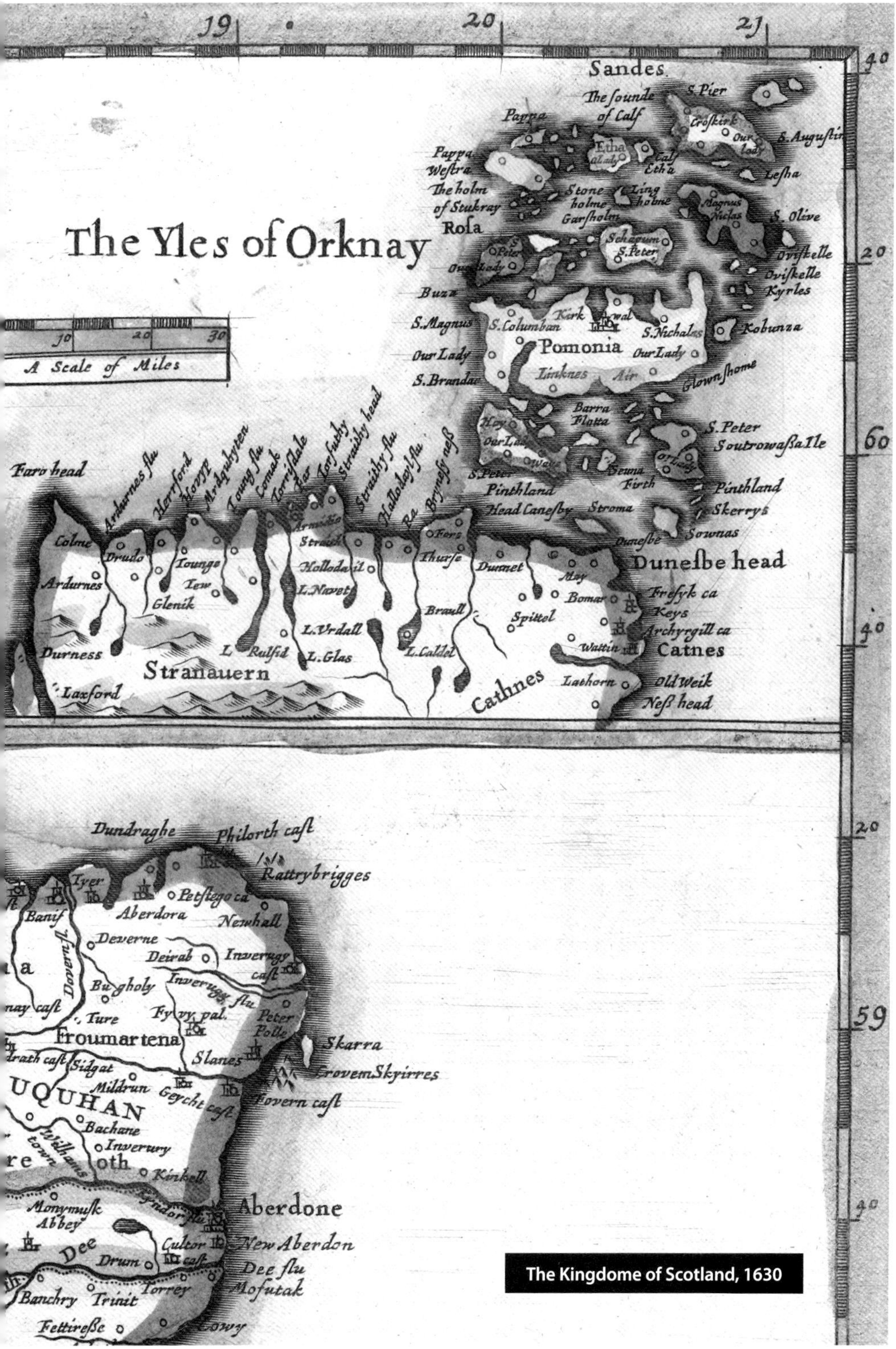

The Kingdome of Scotland, 1630

Index

Entries in **bold** are headings within the text

Publishing Information

Published by the Dorothy Dunnett Society,
Edinburgh, Scotland
Scottish Charity No. SC030649
www.dorothydunnett.org

First edition published by the Dorothy Dunnett Society in 2021

Text: Jenny Myers
Maps: Nicky Cannon
Editor: Heather Jacobson
Series Editor: Jenny Myers
Designer: Suzanne McNeill

ISBN: 978-0-9570046-6-5

Printed and bound by Printwell Limited,
3 Callon Street, Airdrie, ML6 6BW, Scotland.

Photographic and Illustration Credits

Front cover: David Woods/Dreamstime.com (Ring of Brodgar); National Library of Scotland (detail from Gerhard Mercator's *Scotia Regnum*, c. 1595).
Back cover: Jeremy Brown/Dreamstime.com (Brough of Birsay); Bennymarty/Dreamstime.com (Castle Sinclair Girnigoe).

Text pages: Alamy Stock Photo– Chris Jones (55); Rob Sutherland (12r); Realimage (25); Simon Price (69b)
Amelia Cannon (28)
Anne Buchanan (30)
British Museum (3)
Cambridge University Library, MS Ii.6.32, *The Book of Deer*, 5r (67)
Dreamstime.com – Anastasia Yakovleva (59); Cyclingscot (29); Giuseppemasci (11, 12l); H368k742 (37); Jiri Vondrous (43); John Holmes (69t); Klodien (47); Lindamore (1); Stefano Valeri (44t); Wirestock (32)
Geograph.org: Calum McRoberts (38); Colin Smith (44b); David Purchase (31t); James Allan (22b); Lis Burke (34); Mike Searle (72); Richard Webb (65r); Roger Davies (60); Sandy Gerrard (18t); Stanley Howe (73b, 74); Stephen Elwyn Roddick (22t)
Gilbert Summers/must-see-scotland.com (62)
Heather Jacobson (i)
Historic Environment Scotland (16, 61)
James Lancaster/CastlesFortsBattles.co.uk (73t)
Jan Fergus (5, 17t)
Jenny Myers (46)
National Library of Scotland (78–79)
National Museum of Scotland (24, Image © National Museum of Scotland)
Nina Evans (17b, 18b, 19, 31b, 53)
Sidney Foubister (14)
Suzanne McNeill (48, 51, 52, 54, 56, 57, 64, 65l, 66, 70)
Undiscovered Scotland, www.undiscoveredscotland.co.uk (7)
Wikimedia Commons (39)
(t: top; b: bottom; l: left; r: right)

ALSO AVAILABLE

in our series of guides to locations featured in the novels of Dorothy Dunnett

BRUGES: THE DOROTHY DUNNETT GUIDE

Expanded, updated and completely revised, this second edition of *Bruges: The Dorothy Dunnett Guide* builds on the success of the first edition and is packed with new information and maps.

ICELAND: THE DOROTHY DUNNETT GUIDE

Road journeys, maps and planning tips to enable you to track the route of Nicholas de Fleury and his companions as described in *To Lie With Lions*, and to experience the places they did.

EDINBURGH: THE DOROTHY DUNNETT GUIDE

This guide will enable you to see Edinburgh through the eyes of Lymond and Nicholas, as well as introduce you to the beautiful city in which Dorothy Dunnett lived and worked.

RUSSIA: THE DOROTHY DUNNETT GUIDE

Describes many of the locations which feature in *The Ringed Castle* and *Caprice and Rondo*, both in Moscow and beyond, and enables you to glimpse Russia's golden-domed capital, its towns and its countryside as experienced by Lymond and Nicholas.

The guides include:

- A brief history of the country and the period in which the novels take place
- Descriptions of all the locations, past, present and fictional, featured in the novels, as well as places of interest
- Quotations to remind you of their context within the novels
- Maps drawn specially for the guides, highlighting all the locations
- Detailed accounts of important scenes
- Historical illustrations and maps
- Glossaries and pronunciation guides where appropropriate

For any Dunnett reader planning to visit these locations, or just dreaming of doing so, these are the guides for you.

ORDER FROM
dunnettcentral.org/fondaco

In preparation, Dunnett guides to:
Istanbul, the Scottish Borders, Malta, Venice and London

Dorothy Dunnett Society

If you enjoyed this guide and would like to meet with others who also love the books of Dorothy Dunnett, then the Dorothy Dunnett Society is for you.

Dorothy Dunnett loved talking to her readers and hearing their views. She set up the Dorothy Dunnett Society to make it easier for us to keep in touch with each other and share our thoughts. Members around the world receive *Whispering Gallery*, our quarterly magazine about all things Dunnett, with articles about the characters and sources as well as the history and art of the times in which the books are set. We hold our Dunnett Weekend each April in Scotland, and other Gatherings happen from time to time in many different places. International Dorothy Dunnett Day meetings are held on the second Saturday in November around the world, and are open to non-members too.

Please visit our website to find out more about who we are, what we do and what is happening, and to join a community of like-minded souls who love the books and who love to talk about them whether in person or online.

The Dorothy Dunnett Society is a charity registered in Scotland, number SC030649.

www.dorothydunnett.org
www.tinyurl.com/dunnettbooks | www.biblio.com

Find us on Twitter
@dunnettcentral
www.dorothydunnett.org